"DEEP DIVE, MISTER TULL," CAPTAIN SMITH ORDERED. "MAKE 1,500 FEET."

"Aye, aye, Captain," Tull responded. He watched the clockwise movement of the depth gauge's needle and then turned and caught Smith's eyes. There was no hint he suspected something was wrong.

At 1,300 feet the submarine's rate of descent should have slowed, but it didn't. Then the gauge read 1,400 feet and they were still going down.

"Activate manual override!" Smith barked.

"Override not responding," the diving officer said in a tight voice.

"There's a malfunction somewhere, Captain," Tull said. He could see beads of sweat on Smith's forehead. "We're at eighteen and still—"

"Stand by to blow ballast!" Smith ordered.

"Captain," Tull said, "if we blow ballast we'll shoot up like a cork—"

"And tell the admiral . . ." Smith interrupted in a controlled shout, ". . . tell the admiral we have a problem!"

THE FINEST IN FICTION FROM ZEBRA BOOKS!

HEART OF THE COUNTRY   (2299, $4.50)
by Greg Matthews
Winner of the 26th annual WESTERN HERITAGE AWARD for
Outstanding Novel of 1986! Critically acclaimed from coast to
coast! A grand and glorious epic saga of the American West that
NEWSWEEK Magazine called, "a stunning mesmerizing perfor-
mance," by the bestselling author of THE FURTHER ADVEN-
TURES OF HUCKLEBERRY FINN!
        "A TRIUMPHANT AND CAPTIVATING NOVEL!"
            —KANSAS CITY STAR

CARIBBEE   (2400, $4.50)
by Thomas Hoover
From the author of THE MOGHUL! The flames of revolution
erupt in 17th Century Barbados. A magnificent epic novel of bold
adventure, political intrigue, and passionate romance, in the
blockbuster tradition of James Clavell!
        "ACTION-PACKED . . . A ROUSING READ"
            —PUBLISHERS WEEKLY

MACAU   (1940, $4.50)
by Daniel Carney
A breathtaking thriller of epic scope and power set against a back-
ground of Oriental squalor and splendor! A sweeping saga of passion, power, and betrayal in a dark and deadly Far Eastern
breeding ground of racketeers, pimps, thieves and murderers!
        "A RIP-ROARER"
            —LOS ANGELES TIMES

*Available wherever paperbacks are sold, or order direct from the
Publisher. Send cover price plus 50¢ per copy for mailing and handling to Zebra Books, Dept. 2622, 475 Park Avenue South, New
York, N.Y. 10016. Residents of New York, New Jersey and Pennsylvania must include sales tax. DO NOT SEND CASH.*

A NOVEL BY
CHARLES KOREL

FULL ALERT

ZEBRA BOOKS
KENSINGTON PUBLISHING CORP.

ZEBRA BOOKS

are published by

Kensington Publishing Corp.
475 Park Avenue South
New York, NY 10016

Copyright © 1989 by Irving A. Greenfield

All rights reserved. No part of this book may be reproduced
in any form or by any means without the prior written
consent of the Publisher, excepting brief quotes used in
reviews.

First printing: April, 1989

Printed in the United States of America

JB

1

Norfolk, Virginia

There were three men in the motel room and one corpse.

"Jesus!" Detective Lieutenant Charles Benjamin swore. "This is the third killing in the last five days with the same MO." He looked down at the bloodstained body of a young man in his early twenties whose throat had been cut, his genitals severed and stuffed in his mouth. "And no goddamn ID?" he questioned, shifting his eyes to the uniform who had called in the homicide. Benjamin, a burly man with a red face, green eyes muddied by twenty years of looking at the results of violent crimes, had a pronounced southern accent.

"Just a John Doe," the uniform responded. He also had a southern accent, though not as pronounced as Benjamin's.

"How did you get here?" Benjamin asked, running his hand through his wispy gray hair.

"Came over the car radio," the uniform answered. "The dispatcher said an altercation was taking place at the Sea View Motel in room 106. When I got here, the door was closed and everything was quiet. I knocked a few times and, when no one answered, I tried the knob. The door opened. I went in and found him."

"The killer wanted the body found," Benjamin said. "Just the way he did when he knocked off the two other guys."

The coroner, Dr. Anthony Razzili, moved away from the body and said, "If it was the same MO, the kid was drugged before he was killed. But I can't be sure until I do a complete workup. I'll let you know by—" he looked at his watch. "It's almost midnight now . . . sometime late tomorrow afternoon." Razzili, a New Yorker, who had moved to Norfolk five years before, still retained his New York accent.

Benjamin nodded, pulled out a handkerchief from his back pocket and wiped the perspiration from his forehead. The night was hot. There wasn't even the hint of a breeze coming off the Chesapeake. "How long has he been dead?" he questioned.

"A couple of hours, at the most. Rigor mortis hasn't set in yet."

Benjamin took a step closer to the bed and looked at the corpse. There was a small tattoo of a cat on the upper portion of the man's right arm.

"What's really strange about this one and the other two," Razzili commented, "is that the MO is exactly like the one used by a character in the novel, *The Third Deadly Sin*, by—damn it, the guy's name was just on the tip of my tongue."

"Sanders," the uniform said. "Lawrence Sanders. In the book it was a woman psycho who wasted the guys."

Benjamin's eyes went back to the coroner. "You think a woman killed this one and the other two?"

"I couldn't say about this guy one way or another," Razzili answered. "But the other two didn't have sex before they bought it. Each of them had a full load of semen in him. Besides, like I said, they'd been drugged before they were killed."

"The desk clerk here said that one of the men registered under the name of William Gaston, with a New York driving license and address. Both probably will turn up as phony."

Razzili agreed.

"I checked with the Navy and the Marines," Benjamin said. "But they're not missing anyone." He'd sent the prints of the other two stiffs to the FBI. But they never moved swiftly on John Does.

Another uniform walked into the room. "There's a whole mess of newspaper and TV people outside," he reported.

"Tell them I'll be out in a few minutes to give them a statement," he said.

"What are you going to say to them?" Razzili asked.

"The usual bullshit. That we're on to something and are following it up."

Grinning, Razzili said, "Oh, we're on to something . . . that's for sure!"

"There must be a better way of earning a day's pay and keeping honest at the same time," Benjamin responded.

"Come on, Chuck," Razzili said, using the detective's nickname, "deep down inside of you, you know you love it."

Benjamin pursed his lips. "It's a job," he said, walking toward the open door. Instantly, the bright TV lights went on and microphones were shoved toward his face.

2

"Time for me to go, honey," Commander John Tull said, raising himself on one elbow and looking down at Louise Banner, a thirty-year-old divorcee. He'd met her six months ago, when he'd been transferred from the SSBN-715, a boomer, operating out of Seattle, to *Command One*, whose home port was Norfolk.

She moved her fingers over the side of his face. "I'm going to miss you."

Tull bent down and kissed the top of her nose. "I'll be back before you know it."

"I'll be here," she said, caressing the back of his neck.

He put his lips to hers and kissed her passionately, but purposefully didn't respond to what she'd said. Though he certainly enjoyed her company in and out of bed, he wasn't ready to say anything to her that she might misconstrue as a commitment. He'd survived one failed marriage because of his naval career and several intense love affairs, all of which came to a screeching halt for the same reason. Submariners were away from home for long periods of time and that seemed too hard for the women in his life to deal with.

"Can't you tell me when you'll be coming back?" she questioned.

Tull shook his head. "I can't tell you what I don't know, and even if I did know, I couldn't tell you."

Louise pulled herself up, propped the pillows against the headboard and rested against it. "Other than your name and rank, I've been sleeping with a man I don't know."

Tull laughed. "That's one hell of a discovery to make now!"

"I've been thinking about it for some time," she answered. "But it never really struck me until now. You know everything about me, John. I've told you things I never told anyone else."

"I'm a good listener," he responded, spanning her nipples with his bare hand. Her breasts were beautifully shaped half melons with dark pink areolas and nipples.

"Too good," she answered, pushing her long black hair back over her shoulders.

"Alright, tell me what you want to know," Tull said.

"I don't even know what you do aboard the submarine, or even what submarine you're on."

"But you do know I like to read, listen to classical music and enjoy taking pictures, especially of you nude. And I enjoy making love to you. What else do you want to know?"

"Be serious!"

Tull realized it was time for him to leave the bed. There wasn't any way he could be *serious* in the way that she'd asked him to be. He sat up and planted his feet on the floor. He was a tall, lean man with dark brown hair and green eyes. "I really have to go," he said. "In a few hours we'll be under way."

"Do you want me to wait?" Louise asked. "I mean—"

"That's something I can't decide for you," Tull answered, beginning to dress. "If I said *yes,* that might be totally unfair to you. I'd rather you decide."

"But what do you want?" she pressed.

"I'd like to see you when I return," he said.

For several moments, Louise remained silent. "That's not much for me to hold on to," she told him.

He tucked his shirt into his pants. "Not much," he agreed, "but it's all I can give. I don't want to lie to you."

"I thought we had something important going between us," she said, her voice beginning to quaver slightly.

Tull sat down on the bed and took her hands in his. "It is, as you put it, *important,*" he told her. "And I enjoy being with you, but I'm not going to tell you what to do." He released her hands. "I'm not ready for that yet."

"I love you," Louise said in a low, intense voice.

"And I love you," Tull responded, kissing her forehead. "But that doesn't change anything I said. I'm not going to tell you what to do." He stood up and walked to the door of the bedroom. "I'll let myself out."

She nodded.

11

Tull stood in the bedroom doorway for a moment and looked at her. He wanted to remember the way the light from the lamp on the night table fell across her naked body.

Lieutenant Commander William Forbushe, dressed in khaki, sat at the bar in the cocktail lounge of the Holiday Inn just across from Waterside, the city's centerpiece for its urban development program. Though Forbushe lived in a two-and-a-half-room apartment just across the city line in Virginia Beach, he frequented the cocktail lounge because it was a good place to meet women. Secretaries from the Waterside office buildings and those closer to the motel stopped there for a drink and snack during the "cocktail hour," which lasted during the weekdays from 5 P.M. to 7 P.M. And on Saturday night there was usually a good jazz combo playing.

Because it was a Sunday night, the lounge was almost empty. The few people who were there took advantage of the panoramic view of the river offered by a large window opposite the bar.

Forbushe, who was alone, was more interested in the 11 o'clock news than the riverscape behind him. The newscaster, a good-looking black woman, said, "This killing is the third in five days in the Norfolk area. Though details are scanty at this time, the killing, according to an unidentified source in the coroner's office, closely resembles the other two. This means that not only was the victim murdered, but his body was mutilated in the grossest manner. The police say that they are actively pursuing several different avenues of investigation. But so far they have not found the killer. This is Sally Hampton, for Channel Three's Eleven O'clock News. And now to the international scene . . ."

Forbushe downed his Dewars, and catching the barkeeper's eye, he said, "Eddie, give me the same."

"You got it," Eddie answered.

By 1 A.M. Forbushe would be aboard *Command One*, an Ohio class boomer that had been completely modified to be the first underwater electronic command center for a combination of naval, air and amphibious operations. In her cigar-shaped hull, she carried the state-of-the-art computer and communication systems. With these, the admirals and generals in command of an operation could on a moment-by-moment basis direct the movement of ships, planes and men against an enemy. The multiplicity of factors that were involved in making the D-Day landings on the beaches of Normandy on June the 6th, 1944, could be dealt with by the various systems aboard the *Command One* without utilizing its complete capacity. It would still be able to process data from a second operation equal in size and scope to the initial action. As the boat's engineering officer, it was his responsibility to make sure all of its various systems functioned properly, which was one of the reasons why she was going out for a shakedown cruise with an admiral, a Marine general and their staffs aboard. There was even going to be an air operations coordinator along with them.

"Dewars on the rocks," Eddie said, setting the glass down on the bar. "That's really something about those three guys, isn't it?"

"Something," Forbushe responded before he drank.

"A guy was saying here at the bar earlier that killer not only sliced off the kid's dick, but he stuffed it in his mouth."

"Just one or all three?" Forbushe asked.

Eddie shrugged. "I think he was talking about the one that was found today."

Forbushe took another swallow of his drink before he commented, "You really have to watch your prick these days with the possibility of everything happening to it, from getting a case of the clap to having it sliced off and stuck in your mouth."

Eddie shuddered. "Just thinking about it gives me a pain down there."

"I know what you mean," Forbushe said. "I get the same feeling when I see a guy get kneed in the groin in a flick. I always react down there." He finished his drink and looked toward the tables where the late-night patrons were sitting. "Tourists?"

"Yeah. They'll sit there nursing one drink until closing," Eddie said. "Give me the regulars anytime."

"You mean boozers?"

"Nah, though they're where the money is. But a guy like yourself who comes in here a few times a week and spends a few bucks."

"How much do I owe?" Forbushe asked, digging into his pocket for his money clip. He was a swarthy, short, narrow-boned man with coal-black eyes and black hair, which he wore short.

14

Eddie held up five fingers.

"Ten and you take two from the change," Forbushe told him.

"Thanks," Eddie answered, and turning to the cash register, he said, "Tuesday evening there's going to be a fashion show here. Stuff you wouldn't buy your wife, but maybe you'd get one or two things for your girlfriend." He came back to the bar and put three singles down on it.

"I'll try to make it," Forbushe lied, knowing that by that time he'd be into the mission.

"I'll introduce you to a couple of the models," Eddie said.

"I know that will cost me," Forbushe said, getting off the high-back stool.

Eddie grinned. "Nah, not for a friend."

Captain Donald Smith, *Command One*'s skipper, stood in the dining room with his back toward the sliding glass door that looked out on the patio and beyond it, a stretch of dark lawn and swimming pool. "This is one hell of a time to tell me you want out of the marriage," he said, trying hard to remain calm.

"This isn't easy for me," Peggy said. She was seated at the foot of the dining-room table. "But it's the best time for me to leave. It would be much harder if you were here."

Though he silently agreed with her, Smith said nothing. He was a tall, lean man with high cheekbones and graying hair.

"By the time you come back," Peggy told him,

"you'll have all the necessary legal papers from my attorney."

"Are you sure—"

"I'm not sure of anything," Peggy erupted, toying with her fingers. She was a petite blonde, whose figure, despite the fact her next birthday would bring her to the big five-O, was still good.

"Did you have anything to drink before you decided to tell me you're leaving?" Smith asked. Like many Navy wives, she had developed a "drinking problem" that would often manifest itself before he'd leave on a cruise.

"Why must you always ask that same question whenever I tell you something?" she asked, her voice rising to the edge of a scream.

Smith didn't answer. He shouldn't have asked the question. This wasn't the time to have another discussion about her drinking.

"I'll write the children and explain what's going on," she said. "They're old enough to understand that things like this sometime happen."

"Why don't you wait until I return?" Smith suggested, softening his tone. "It will give you more time to think about the situation and it will do the same for me."

"I've had time to think about it," Peggy answered. "God, I've had time. Years! Besides, once you're on your boat, you won't think about anything but your command. No, I've done as much thinking about this as I can possibly do. This is the best way I know to bring to an end something that really ended a long time ago."

Smith shifted his weight from his right foot to his

left. "I guess then," he said in a low voice, "you should do what you've decided to do. But I still think there's room for some discussion between us."

Peggy shook her head.

The sound of a car stopping in front of the house brought a sudden silence between them.

"My cab," Smith said.

Peggy stood up. "Take care of yourself, Don," she told him.

He started for the door.

"Aren't you taking anything?" she asked.

"Everything of mine is already aboard," he answered as he stopped and faced her. "Take care of yourself, Peggy."

"Yes, I'll try," she said in a choked voice.

Smith pursed his lips. This would be the first time he'd leave her without kissing her goodbye. He waited a moment. If she'd make the slightest movement toward him, he'd go to her. But she didn't.

"I'll let you know where I am," Peggy said.

"Have you enough money?" he asked.

"Yes."

Silently they faced each other; then, with a nod, Smith turned, set his cap on his head, opened the door and stepped out into the warm humid night. Moments later he settled into the back of the cab and told the driver where to go.

Tull swung his Honda Civic wagon into a 7-Eleven parking lot, slowed and came to a stop.

Almost immediately, the store's door opened and

17

a heavyset man wearing blue slacks, a white polo shirt and carrying a 7-Eleven paper bag, walked out.

Tull leaned across the front seat and opened the door. "Waiting long, Harry?" he asked.

Harry settled next to him and closed the door before answering, "Five minutes. I bought a couple of containers of coffee and two of those Drake's coffee cakes, the kind with the crumbs on top."

Tull pulled out of the parking lot and, smiling, he said, "If your libido was as active as your sweet tooth, you'd fuck yourself into the grave instead of eating your way there."

"Do you want the coffee and cake?" Harry asked, opening the top of the bag.

"Coffee. I hope you didn't put sugar and cream in it," Tull said.

"I got yours black, no sugar."

Tull took the container from him.

"Have you heard the news?" Harry asked.

"No. I didn't have the radio on."

"You have your tenth man," Harry said. "He should be reporting aboard about now. Each will identify himself by giving you a piece of a puzzle. When you put all of the pieces together they will form a capital T. Like it?"

Tull didn't respond to the question. But he asked one of his own. "Suppose there's a plant? An eleventh man would make the ten others suspect."

"It's possible that eleven men will identify themselves, but not very probable," Harry answered, taking a bite of the coffee cake.

"Was this one done the way the others were?"

18

Tull asked.

Harry slowly chewed the coffee cake before he answered, "Yeah, it's going to confuse the hell out of them, and by the time they have it sorted out and put together, it will be too late for them to do anything about it. Besides, it had a psychological purpose. It scares the shit out of other men when they hear about it, or read about it. Every man values his cock more than any other part of his anatomy."

"Three with the same MO happening within a span of a few days puts a lot of pressure where we don't want pressure," Tull said, stopping for a red light. He drank more of the coffee.

"When this is over, what are you going to do?" Harry questioned.

"Haven't thought about it," Tull responded, putting the car in motion as soon as the light went green.

"Well, my work is done," Harry said contentedly. "By noon tomorrow, I'll be far away."

Tull finished the coffee and put the empty container back in the bag.

"I'll be glad to leave this place," Harry said. "It's too damn bland for my tastes. I guess I'm just a big city boy after all."

As they approached the base gate, Tull slowed, then stopped. A young Marine stepped out of the guard house.

Tull flashed his ID.

The Marine stepped back and saluted.

Returning the courtesy, Tull eased down on the accelerator.

"Doesn't it give you an odd feeling every time you

19

do that?" Harry asked.

"I've been doing it so long that it has become second nature to me," Tull answered.

"Are you getting along any better with the captain?" Harry asked.

Tull glanced at Harry in the rearview mirror. In the months that he'd known him, he'd never really decided what he thought about him and now was too late to think about him. "He asked for the XO off his last command and got me instead. In his shoes, I'd have been pissed too. But we've learned to dance around each other."

Harry dug into his side pocket and pulled out a small black metal case, no larger than a calling card, and tearing the Velcro seal, he opened it. "There are enough here to do the job," he said.

Tull glanced at it. There were thirty-five white plastic rings, arranged in seven rows. They looked like reinforcements for loose-leaf paper, "What are they?"

"A synthetic variation of rattlesnake venom. It will make a man sick enough to think he's dying, but he won't. A light pressure, less than a twentieth of an ounce, pushes the substance into the skin and in a matter of minutes, two at the most, the body's circulatory system does the rest. The effects last anywhere from twenty to forty-eight hours, depending on the individual and other circumstances."

"Give me the other circumstances," Tull said as they drove by the aircraft carriers *Nimetz* and *America*.

"The effect is more severe and lasts longer if the recipient is in a state of emotional distress."

"This has been verified by tests?"

"Absolutely," Harry responded.

"I'll think of something," Tull assured him.

Harry closed the case and sealed it by pressing the Velcro strips between his fingers. "All yours," he said. And then he took out a pack of cigarettes. "The antidote is in here. It works very quickly."

"Give me a number."

"Ten minutes," Harry answered, handing him his cigarette pack.

Tull slipped it into his right trouser pocket. "We're coming up to the barrier," he said. In front of them there were several large concrete blocks caught in the glare of the headlights, and on either side of the road was a guard house. "Remember," he said, "when you leave the base, you drive back to my place the way I showed you. No shortcuts and no stops."

"And move at an even forty miles per," Harry laughed.

"That's absolutely right."

"Until I worked with you, I thought I was a cautious man," Harry said. "You have me beat by a mile."

Tull didn't answer.

"Well, John, as the saying goes, I can't say that it hasn't been interesting," Harry said, offering his hand. "I'm sorry that our paths will never cross again."

"Me too," Tull replied, shaking his hand; then he slowed the car and brought it to a stop in front of the first barrier.

A Marine guard came out of the guard house on the left side and asked Tull for identification, while a second Marine guard pointed an M-16 at them.

"Commander John Tull," Tull said.

The Marine on the left stepped back into the guard house, picked up a phone, spoke a few words, listened and, putting the phone down, he said, "You're clear, Commander."

"Thank you," Tull answered, and opening the door, he said to Harry, "You take it from here."

"Good luck!"

Tull nodded and left the car. He waited until Harry put the car in reverse and completed a U-turn before he started the long walk to the end of the last pier, where *Command One* was tied up.

Harry exited the base through the same gate that Tull had entered and immediately turned right. Within minutes he crossed into the Virginia Beach area and was heading out toward a heavily wooded area that ran parallel to the bay. By tomorrow night he'd be enjoying dinner at his favorite bistro in Paris. The thought made his mouth water. He smiled and, reaching over to the dashboard, he turned on the radio. The next instant there was a tremendous roar. Blood poured from ears, mouth and nose. "Tull," he screamed into the flames. *"Tull!"*

"Stand by fore and aft to cast off lines," Tull ordered over the radio.

"Standing by," each of the chiefs in charge of the detail radioed.

"Standing by to cast off fore and aft lines," Tull

said, looking at the boat's skipper, Captain Donald Smith. The two of them shared the bridge, a narrow, circular well located on top of the thirty-foot sail that housed the boat's various radar and communication antennas.

"Gangway off," Smith said.

"Gangway off," Tull ordered.

Instantly, the detail amidships lifted the gangway off the deck and rolled it back on the pier.

"Gangway clear," Tull announced as soon as the report came over the radio.

Smith turned and looked out over the stern, where the boat's slowly idling propeller churned the water. He faced the bow again. "Cast off all lines," he said.

Tull radioed the order and, a few moments later, he reported, "All lines away."

"Standard rudder. Back, one third," Smith said.

Tull repeated the order and relayed it to the boat's control room. Within a matter of moments the boat's screw changed direction and as *Command One* began to ease backward toward the dark, open expanse of the Chesapeake, the floodlights on the pier went out.

Smith reached over to the small control panel and switched on the boat's running lights. "All deck details below," he said.

Tull nodded and transmitted the order.

Smith scanned the immediate area with infrared glasses. "Nothing close by," he commented, handing the glass to Tull.

"Nothing," Tull confirmed, after making a slow 360 search. "Do you want me to double check with radar?" he asked.

23

Smith shook his head. Radar had a standing order to report any target within a thousand yards of the boat whenever she left or entered a port.

Command One moved into midchannel.

"All engines stop," Smith ordered. "Left full rudder."

Tull gave the directions to the control room.

The boat's movement slowed and her bow began to swing around toward the south.

"Ahead, one third," Smith ordered.

"Ahead, one third," Tull told the control room.

"Come to course seven five," Smith said.

"Course seven five," Tull repeated.

Command One headed toward the lower bay.

Smith helped himself to a cigarette and offered one to Tull. "I forgot that you're a nonsmoker." Shielding the flame from a cigarette lighter, he lit up and blew out a cloud of smoke, before he said, "It's going to take some work to turn the men on board into a crew."

"This shakedown will help," Tull answered.

"A quarter of this bunch is straight out of sub school," Smith said. "And, like yourself, all of the officers are off different boats. None of you have worked together."

"I'm sure everyone will give you his best," Tull responded, aware that Smith lacked his usual air of self-assurance.

"Yes, I'm sure they will. I've already seen that in you and several others," Smith told him.

"Thank you, sir," Tull said.

"I just wanted you to know that I appreciate your work."

"I couldn't do anything unless the men were willing to cooperate," Tull said modestly. "The credit belongs to every man aboard. I believe you'll quickly find that you have the best crew you've ever had."

Smith flashed a boyish smile. "I think so too," he said, taking a last drag on the cigarette before he flicked it into the white foam that ran along *Command One*'s side.

3

Tull had the conn. *Command One*, or *C-1* in the Navy's nomenclature, was cruising at thirty-five knots five hundred feet below the Atlantic, three hundred miles east of Wilmington, North Carolina. All systems were functioning normally. The men on watch in the control room kept conversation to a minimum.

Tull checked the clock. It was 11:30. At 11:45 they were scheduled to make a routine radio check with COMSUBLANT in Norfolk. Glancing at the diving officer, Lieutenant Keith Howard, he said, "Diving Officer, come to periscope antenna depth."

"Aye, aye, sir," Howard answered, and immediately ordered an upward angle on the diving planes, followed by another set of orders that sequenced the opening and closing of valves replacing seawater in the main ballast tanks with air.

C-1 responded. Her bow lifted.

Tull looked at the inclinometer. They were moving up at 10 degrees. His eyes went to the depth gauge. They were already passing through the 400-

foot level.

Forbushe entered the control room, nodded and crossed over to where the sonar and radar operators were located. In the event that *C-1* became involved in an action against enemy submarines, this area would become the Command Decision Center, the CDC, and the skipper would fight the battle from there. But there was another CDC located on the "flag bridge," an area just below the control room, where the admiral and general in command of an invasion force would direct the ships, planes and men involved in the evolution. This CDC was the real reason for the existence of *C-1*. It was equipped to display on three large screens all the surface and submarine forces within an operating radius of one hundred nautical miles, all aircraft within a range of three hundred nautical miles and the disposition of ground forces within a hundred miles. This information was obtained from flyovers by surveillance aircraft and satellite specially equipped to transmit data to the *C-1*. In addition, American warships and submarines involved in an operation would constantly supply information via coded transmissions. The disposition of American troops and enemy troops would be constantly monitored by aircraft and choppers, enabling the general onboard the *C-1* to field his troops more effectively than would have previously been possible.

"Coming to periscope depth," Howard announced.

Tull waited a few moments until the boat was level before he raised the periscope and the ESM (electronic support measures) antenna. With his eyes pressed against the periscope's eyepiece, Tull made a 360. The surface was calm and empty in every direction for the full range of the periscope. The sun was shining and the sky was blue, with a few puffs of clouds to the west. "Nice day up there," he commented aloud; then, moving away from the periscope, he checked the ESM instruments for radar emissions. Nothing. He raised the UHF (ultrahigh frequency) receiving antenna and a laser transmitter that locked on to the communication satellite. Used only by submarines, this combination enabled them to send longer messages without revealing their position.

"Stand by to transmit," Tull said.

"Standing by," the radioman answered.

Tull watched the clock. The instant it read 11:45 he said, "Transmit."

The radioman touched the signal button. Within moments he received an answer and, checking it against the one he'd sent, he reported, "Signal copied, sir."

Tull lowered the periscope and all of the other masts. "Diving Officer, make five hundred feet," he said.

"Aye, aye, sir," Howard answered.

Tull's eyes automatically went to the depth gauge. *C-1* had a quick response time to diving and surfacing commands. She was already down at the bow.

Forbushe stopped alongside Tull. "Everything looks good."

Tull continued to stare at the depth gauge. They were passing through 150 feet. "The T is complete," he said.

"I was wondering when you would tell me," Forbushe responded.

Annoyed with the man's sarcasm, Tull gave him a sideways glance, but didn't say anything.

"I'm ready whenever you are."

"We have a set timetable," Tull answered. "You know the drill, and we're going to stay with it."

Expressionless, except for a sudden ignition of light in his coal-black eyes, Forbushe nodded and silently walked away.

Tull continued to look at the diving gauge. He was less than pleased with having to work with Forbushe and he was sure that the feeling was mutual.

"Five hundred feet, conn," Howard reported.

"On the mark," Tull answered; then turning to the DO, he gave him a thumbs-up.

After his watch, Tull was in his bunk with his hands behind his head. He wasn't asleep. But his eyes were closed. Of all the missions he had undertaken, this was by far the most dangerous. From the very beginning, he didn't like having to work with Forbushe or Harry—Harry, the poor son of a bitch hadn't the foggiest notion that as soon as he'd killed the third kid in the motel room, he'd be excess baggage that couldn't be carried. "But Forbushe is a different matter," he whispered to himself. The man was a zealot and he never knew a zealot who wasn't a dangerous man.

Tull took a deep breath and slowly exhaled. When this operation was over, he intended to "put in his papers," so to speak. He was forty years old, and for the last fifteen years of his life, he'd been involved with characters like Forbushe and Harry. Maybe he'd go back to Louise and have some sort of meaningful relationship. In or out of bed they seemed to have something going between them. Something that might—

The phone on the bulkhead next to his bunk rang. Tull fully opened his eyes and, before it rang a second time, he reached over, took the phone off the hook and said, "Commander Tull here."

"Commander, the skipper wants to see you in his office," the yeoman said.

Tull recognized the voice. "Good or bad, Steve?" he asked.

"Routine, I'd say," Steve answered.

Tull thanked him, replaced the phone on the bulkhead and put his shoes back on; then, pausing at the small steel sink on the other side of the cabin, he washed and dried his face before he left to see the captain.

Forbushe sat behind a small desk in a cubbyhole in the after section of the boat, between the reactor compartment and the engine room. The bulkheads were bare, except for a twelve-month calendar with a crotch shot of a lovely-looking blonde so detailed that moisture glistened on the hairs of her vaginal lips. There was a computer terminal to his right on the desk and a second one behind him. The one on the desk provided him with immediate access to the installation, operation, repair manuals and parts

31

lists for every piece of electronic gear on the *C-1*. Using a series of macro commands of his own devising, he was able to instantly put on the screen the necessary information to service any of the electronic devices on board and with a laser printer immediately translate it to hard text for use by the technicians. The computer situated behind him was tied into the *C-1*'s main frame and provided him with the operating condition of the boat's operating systems and it was also tied to the damage-control system net which permitted him to help the damage-control officer in the event of a problem.

Forbushe was totally aware of how important he was to the smooth functioning of the *C-1*. He was also very much aware of how important he was to the mission, and he resented Tull for not treating him as an equal. The success of the mission depended as much upon him as it did upon Tull. There wasn't any real reason why Control had put Tull in charge. None. Forbushe helped himself to a cigarette from the pack lying on the desk, lit it and blew smoke toward the open door. As far as he was concerned, the operation should begin as soon as possible. He took another drag on the cigarette. When the time came, Tull would have to do things his way, or he'd have to have him removed. There were ten other men involved in the mission, and though each of them was still unknown to him, he had absolutely no doubt that among them there were several who would give him a royal flush if he had to outpoker Tull.

The phone rang.

Forbushe identified himself.

"Commander, the skipper wants you to come to his office," Steve said.

"I'm on my way," Forbushe answered, stubbing out his cigarette in a hammered copper ashtray, a souvenir of a visit to Cairo, Egypt, a few years before.

"Yes, sir, I'll tell him," Jones said.

"Gentlemen, please make yourselves comfortable. Smoke if you wish," Smith said, looking at Forbushe.

Tull settled in the chair in front of Smith's desk and Forbushe took the one to the captain's right.

As Smith filled his pipe, he said, "In a few hours we'll be in position to make the first of a series of deep test dives. This one will be to a depth of fifteen hundred feet, which we will maintain for a period of four hours." He tamped down the tobacco in the pipe bowl and lit it. When it was drawing to his satisfaction, he asked, "Do either of you have any comments pro or con?" He looked at Forbushe.

"None, sir."

His eyes went to Tull.

"Are you going to announce the depth before the dive?" Tull asked.

Smith puffed at his pipe. "An announcement might make the green kids jumpy."

"Those in the control room might be more jumpy when you tell the DO to make fifteen hundred feet than when they watch the depth gauge needle move."

Smith blew smoke up at the ceiling. "What's your opinion, Mister Forbushe?"

33

"I'd make the dive without any previous announcement."

"Yes, that's my feeling too. The quicker the new men become used to expecting the unexpected, the more we will be able to depend upon them in an emergency." He looked at Tull again.

"There's no taking issue with that point," Tull said. "Will we be at general quarters when we make the dive?"

"I don't see why we should," Smith answered. "I'll have the con and give the order."

"Would you want me in the control room?"

"No. I think the more we treat this as part of our normal operating procedure, the easier it will be for the new men to treat the deep dives like any other."

Tull nodded and took a quick look around the cabin. Since he'd been assigned to the *C-1*, he had been in it more times than he could remember. It was more spacious than his own or Forbushe's, but not nearly as large as the admiral's. There were several photographs on the bulkheads. One of Smith's wife, who was a good-looking woman, somewhat younger than the skipper. Two of his children. One of his class at the Academy and one of his last command. In addition to the desk, there were two banks of telephones that instantly connected the skipper to any part of the boat; there was the 1MC system, which he could either actuate from the control room, this office, or his cabin, which was through a door on the left. On the right were several computer terminals, two laser printers, sonar and radar CRTs. The computers gave him the same capability as Forbushe had. Should the situation

34

require it, he could direct the repair, or damage control, detail from the office. He could also monitor the presence of any subsurface, surface, or air unknowns without having to go to the control room until he decided to sound general quarters.

"Based on our present speed, position, projected course and required depth," Smith said, typing the two parameters into one of the computers, "we should be in our dive position in—" The value 0:0130 came up on the CRT to the right of a chart showing the present position, their course line to where the ocean floor dropped off from a couple of hundred feet to more than seventeen thousand. "An hour and a half from now . . . Make it two hours, gentlemen," Smith told them.

"How long will we remain at fifteen hundred feet?" Tull asked.

"Four hours."

"On the same heading?"

"Yes," Smith answered. His eyes moved from Tull to Forbushe. "I want tests run on all of our systems."

"Aye, aye, sir."

"Any questions, gentlemen?" Smith asked.

"None," Tull answered.

"None, Captain," Forbushe responded.

4

"My cabin in five minutes," Tull said as soon as they were some distance from the captain's cabin.

Forbushe gave him a questioning look.

"Five minutes," Tull repeated sharply and went to the navigation room to get a firsthand look at the charts of the area where the first deep dive would take place. The chart file was computerized. Each major sea area was subdivided into discrete latitudinal and longitudinal sections of precisely ten east and west and the same number of degrees north and south.

Lieutenant Paul Hacker, the boat's navigation officer, was responsible for maintaining its course and its exact position at any given instant. To achieve this point of accuracy a variety of sophisticated devices were used, including a state-of-the-art inertial guidance system, constant radio checks—even while the boat was submerged with the communications center in upper Michigan and whenever the boat was at periscope depth or on the surface—and instantaneous radio linkage to anyone of two different navigation satellites, depending on where they were operating at the time.

Tull moved to the Present Position Display CRT, which marked *C-1*'s position with a red dot, alongside of which its latitude and longitude were given to the half minute. By punching specific directions on the keyboard, distance to any of six multiple points on the earth's surface would be displayed instantly.

Hacker came up to Tull. "All systems are green," he said with a smile of satisfaction on his boyishly freckled face.

"What's the bottom look like?" Tull answered, glancing at the yeoman off to one side. He was one of the men who'd identified himself with a piece of the puzzle.

"In about ten minutes we'll be off the continental shelf and heading out over the Hatteras Abyssal Plain." Hacker said, moving to another terminal and quickly running his fingers over the keyboard. A three-dimensional view of the bottom came into view. "We've got two arrays of sonar that continually sweep the bottom, and from the return we can digitally convert the echoes to what you see on the screen."

"How far down is bottom of the plain?" Tull asked. The bottom was four hundred feet below them and dropping off, even as he was looking at the screen.

"Seventeen thousand plus," Hacker answered.

"Can you get as good a picture of it as you have on the screen now?"

"Not as detailed."

Tull nodded, thanked him and headed for his cabin. Moments later Forbushe entered it without knocking.

"Can you create an accident?" Tull asked, sitting down at his small desk and gesturing to Forbushe to take the empty chair.

"I prefer to stand," Forbushe said. "Now tell me what the hell you're talking about?"

Tull understood the psychological advantage that Forbushe hoped to gain by standing and stood up. "I'm talking about an accident that would not be fatal to any member of the crew or to the boat during the deep dive, but would scare the hell out everyone."

Forbushe frowned.

"Until we move, I want a series of them," he said. He had no intention of explaining why. The less Forbushe knew, the easier his mission would be.

"Things could be made to happen," Forbushe answered.

"For openers, can you maintain the dive beyond fifteen hundred feet?"

"How much deeper?"

"Close to maximum design depth."

"Probably."

"I want a definite yes or no. A probably might send us to the bottom and that will be seventeen thousand feet."

Forbushe brushed his arm across his forehead. "I don't like it. It's too damn dangerous."

"That's exactly why it must be done," Tull said. "The distance to the bottom will scare the shit out of Smith."

"Suppose something goes wrong. I mean really wrong and we keep going down?"

"Then we're dead," Tull said coldly. "But what I need to know from you is how probable is your probably?"

Shifting his weight from one foot to another, Forbushe said, "Christ, I'm going to be fucking with the ballast system. At that depth, almost anything might happen."

"Alright, you give me a depth."

"Two k."

"That's only five hundred feet below—"

"I give you a definite yes at that depth," Forbushe said.

Tull reached over to the desk and lifted a cigarette out of the pack, lit it and, looking straight at Forbushe, he said, "Take it down to three k. That's where it will have the most effect and that's where I want it."

"But the risk—"

"Three k," Tull said, his voice hard and the look in his eyes ever harder.

Forbushe hesitated, then nodded.

"I'll pass the word to our men," Tull said. "I don't want them unnecessarily rattled."

"Anything else?" Forbushe questioned.

Shaking his head, Tull said, "Just make sure we don't go to the bottom."

Forbushe glared at him, turned and, without a word, he left the cabin.

Taking a deep drag on the cigarette, Tull blew a cloud of smoke toward the cabin's low ceiling.

The more dangerous the situation, the more the men would be afraid, the quicker the drug would work.

Smith was on the flag bridge, where the boat's Command Decision Center was located. Admiral Gromly, a bear of a man of fifty-five, was responsible for the *C-1* coming into being. With him was Marine Corps Brigadier General Peter Hass, who had seen three tours of combat duty during the war in Vietnam in the sixties and early seventies.

"We'll cruise at the depth of fifteen hundred feet for a period of four hours," Smith told the two officers. "That will give your staff enough time to make whatever tests they deem necessary."

Looking at Hass, Gromly nodded. "That's fine with me. What about you, General?"

Hass nodded. He was a rangily built man with sharp angular features and dark gray eyes. "I'm just a guest," he said with a smile. "I'll go where you take me, Captain."

The three of them were sitting at a small table that had one side secured to the bulkhead. Suddenly one of the CDC's phones rang and an officer on the admiral's staff answered it.

"Captain, it's for you," the officer said.

Smith excused himself, left the table and, stepping up to the bank of phones, took ahold of the one held out to him.

"Captain, we're picking up two Victors on our passive, bearing two eight zero, range twenty thousand yards, speed two eight and closing."

"Positive ID?" Smith answered.

"Yes, sir."

"I'm on my way to the control center," Smith said and, replacing the phone in its cradle on the bank, he returned to the table. "We've got two Victors closing in on us. Probably to take a look at us."

"How close are you going to let them come?" Gower asked.

"Close enough to let them wonder where we went, when we go," Smith said and headed for the control room, where the sonar officer was looking at two red targets on the sonar display terminal.

"Speed has increased to thirty knots and still closing," the officer reported.

He nodded, moved to the other side of the control room and, with his forefinger, depressed a red button. A thirty-second shriek on the klaxon sent the crew running to their battle stations. He pressed the 1MC button. "Battle Stations . . . All hands, battle stations."

Tull came dashing into the control room.

"Two Victors closing fast," Smith said. "Stand by for fire control mission."

"Aye, aye, Captain," Tull answered and relayed the order to the fire control officer.

"Assume presence of one attack sub three thousand yards in front, two hundred feet above us and moving at thirty-two knots."

"Aye, aye, sir," the fire control officer answered, already cranking the position and speed of the screening attack submarine into the fire-control computer.

Instantaneously the computer screen displayed

the position of the two Victors, the *C-1* and the imaginary attack submarine relative to each other and, in a matter of moments, the computer indicated the change of course for the attack submarine that would bring it on an intercept course with the two Victors. Then it proceeded to continuously solve the fire-control problem from the attack submarine to the Russian submarines. Had this been a real fire-control problem instead of a simulation, then the solutions would have been exactly the same as those shown on the attack submarine's fire-control computer.

The officer at the fire-control computer began to call out values for depth, bow angle and time to target.

"Secure from fire-control mission," Smith ordered.

"Secure from fire-control mission," Tull repeated.

"Fire-control mission secured," the FCO responded.

"All engines, ahead full speed," Smith ordered.

"All engines ahead answered," the engine-room signal man said, responding to the green indication on the engine-control panel.

"Helmsman, come to course two five," Smith said.

"Coming to course two five," the helmsman answered.

Smith moved back to the sonar display. The distance between the two Russian submarines and the *C-1* had already made itself apparent on the screen.

Tull came up alongside him. "The skippers of

those Victors are going to wonder what the hell they came in contact with," he said, looking at the scope.

Smith turned to him and grinned. "That's the way to give them proverbial shits." Then he laughed loudly.

Tull, Hacker and everyone else who heard him laughed too.

"There probably will be half a dozen of them waiting for us when we return," Tull commented.

"Yeah, I guess there will," Smith said. He looked at the scope again. "They've gone to flank." He looked sideways at Tull. "But it won't help them."

"We go up to flank and those skippers will really have the nervous runs."

"What the hell, why not!" Smith exclaimed and ordered, "Flank speed."

"Flank speed answered," the engine-room signal man responded.

Smith moved back to the center of the control room and motioned Tull to follow him. "Might as well go into our first deep dive," he said.

"There's a hell of a lot of water under us," Tull remarked. He looked up at the fathometer. "Make it about sixteen hundred."

"Targets off the scope," the SO reported.

"Six boats waiting for us when we return," Tull said.

"Odds?"

"Nine to five."

Smith shook his head. "I have an idea. We'll have a pool. Each man will select the number of Ruskie boats he thinks will be waiting for us when we return. Guessing the right number pays off."

"What's the pot?"

"We've got a crew of forty—say five bucks a man. Two hundred isn't a bad pot."

"What about Admiral Gromly and General Hass and their staffs. That would almost double it."

"I'll ask them whether they want to be in it. A pool like that will go a long way toward creating a real team," Smith commented.

Tull agreed.

"Deep dive, Mister Tull," Smith said.

"Aye, aye, Captain."

"Diving Officer, make fifteen hundred feet," Smith ordered.

The DO shot a glance at Smith before he responded, "Making fifteen hundred feet." Immediately there was the familiar sound of valves opening and seawater rushing into the ballast tanks.

"All engines ahead two thirds," Smith said.

The signalman acknowledged the change in the boat's speed.

"Five hundred feet," the DO said.

Tull watched the clockwise movement of the depth gauge's needle and every few moments flicked his eyes to the green digital readout of the electronic depth gauge.

The boat was dropping through the water very fast. At increments of fifty feet the DO called out the depth.

Tull caught Smith's eyes. There was no hint that he suspected something was wrong.

"Twelve hundred feet," the DO reported; then to the men at the emergency ballast controls, he said, "Stand by!" Aboard the *C-1*, the amount and position of the ballast in ballast tanks was electronically calculated and controlled based on the depth. In the event that the automatic system failed, the men at the ballast controls would activate the manual backup system.

At thirteen hundred feet, the boat's rate of descent should have begun to slow. But it didn't.

"System check?" Smith called out.

"Normal," the DO responded.

The depth gauge read fourteen hundred feet and they were still going down.

"Activate manual override!" Smith barked. "All engines ahead one third."

The engine-room signal man responded, "All engines ahead one third answered."

"Manual override activated."

Tull could see the beads of sweat on Smith's forehead.

"Fourteen fifty," the DO called out.

"All engines stop," Smith ordered.

The engine-room signal man responded with, "All engines stopped, sir."

The control room was absolutely silent except for the hissing sound made by the air being displaced by water in the ballast tanks.

"Trim to the mark," the DO ordered.

Tull kept his eyes on the depth gauge. The boat reached fifteen hundred feet and was still going down.

"Override not responding," the DO reported in a tight voice.

Smith went to a bank of phones. "Damage control auto-dive system malfunctioned. Manual unable to

46

override." He looked toward Tull. "DC hasn't any malfunction indication."

"There sure as hell is a malfunction somewhere," Tull responded. "We're eighteen down and still—"

"Stand by to blow all ballast!" Smith ordered, his voice a controlled shout.

Another phone rang.

Tull answered; then, putting his hand over the mouthpiece, he said, 'The admiral's watch officer says he thought the test dive depth was fifteen hundred feet. He has a depth reading of eighteen hundred and still going down."

"Tell him—"

"Two thousand feet," the DO called out.

Smith took a deep breath and slowly exhaled. "Tell the admiral's WO we have a problem."

Suddenly Gromly came into the control room. "What the hell is going on?" he demanded.

"Two thousand and fifty feet," the DO reported.

Gromly frowned; then, as the realization of what was happening took hold, he paled. "Manual override—"

Smith shook his head.

"My God, there's thousands of feet of water under us!" Gromly exclaimed.

"If we blow ballast, we'll shoot up like a cork and probably damage the hull's outer skin and—"

Suddenly the hissing sound of the air leaving the ballast tanks stopped and was replaced by the whir of pumps.

There was a gentle upward movement.

The depth gauge needle quivered, stopped at two thousand and seventy-five feet and began to move counterclockwise.

"Secure manual override system," the DO ordered.

"All engines ahead two thirds," Smith said.

The engine-room signal man acknowledged the command.

"Eighteen hundred feet, and still moving up," the DO reported.

"Well," Gromly said, "at my age I could have done without that experience." He managed a smile.

"I'm sure every man aboard has the same thought, Admiral," Smith responded. "Let's hope it's an isolated incident. But we won't know that until we make another deep dive."

Gromly nodded. "And we look at the systems tapes when we return to Norfolk."

"Fifteen hundred feet and trimmed to the mark," the DCO reported.

"We'll maintain this depth for the next four hours, as planned," Smith said, looking at Tull.

"Aye, aye, Captain," Tull answered.

After the *C-1* completed its first deep dive test, Smith prepared a report of the incident and transmitted it via satellite to COMSUBLANT, Norfolk, Virginia. Then with Forbushe, Tull and the Damage Control Officer, Lieutenant Commander Thomas, along with him, he made a personal inspection of as much of the auto-diving system as was visible. But more than half of the system consisted of electronically activated pressure valves and other types of sensors located inside the ballast

48

tanks or in the maze of piping between them. What he saw, he found in excellent operating condition.

When the party returned to the control room, Forbushe said, "Sir, I'm beginning to think that it was an anomalous condition."

Smith repeated the word "anomalous," and said, "That fucking condition, if it shows up again, could kill all of us, Mister Forbushe." Then in a less hostile tone, he said, "I don't want any more of that kind of condition aboard my boat."

"Yes, sir," Forbushe answered.

Smith looked at his watch. "It's just about twilight topside," he said. "We'll surface and by zero four hundred rendezvous with our battle group. By zero six-thirty tomorrow morning we'll be involved in sea maneuvers."

Tull glanced at Forbushe. This was a new twist. "Sir," he said, turning to Smith, "are we to understand that the *C-1* will be part of a battle group exercise?"

Smith grinned. "That and more," he answered.

Tull suddenly realized that explained the presence of Gromly and Hass aboard. Had they been going on just an ordinary shakedown cruise, neither of them would have been needed. He was annoyed with himself for not having understood the real meaning of their presence.

"We're part of the Blue Strike Force, actually the command ship, and our forces will make a landing on an uninhabited island south of Puerto Rico and it will be opposed by the Red Force."

"It will certainly test the boat's ability to act as the command center," Bright commented.

"Absolutely," Smith responded, and then asked if any one of them had a question. "None? Good. We'll surface in twenty minutes. That's it for now, men. Dismissed."

"Mister Forbushe, may I see you for a moment," Tull said as they left the control room.

Forbushe slowed his pace.

"My cabin," Tull said.

Moments later they were secure behind a closed door.

"Just how the hell are we going to get this boat out from under a whole goddamn battle group?" Forbushe questioned almost angrily. "I mean whoever goofed on this one, really goofed."

Tull agreed and, helping himself to a cigarette from the open pack on the desk, he said, "It certainly tightens the timetable."

"What the hell are you talking about?" Forbushe asked, flinging himself down into the chair next to the desk.

"We don't rendezvous for almost a full twelve hours," Tull said, blowing smoke out of his nostrils and sitting down on the edge of the desk. "That means we have twelve hours of time and the equivalent amount of ocean to get lost in."

Forbushe looked at him questioningly.

"Suppose a man is murdered aboard—"

"Cm'on, that's really wild!" Forbushe exclaimed, getting to his feet.

Tull pointed the cigarette at him. "It would make everyone nervous, wouldn't it. More nervous than they might be if the first test dive hadn't become an 'anomalous' situation. Someday, you'll have to

50

explain to me just how you managed to accomplish that."

"Easy, once you know what to short out, including the malfunction indications on the damage control net. But now—"

"Listen," Tull said, "you did one hell of a job. Now we've got to get this thing done. A dead man will mean having a chopper come to pick up the body, and if the chopper meets with an accident in plain sight of the *C-1*, everyone's nerves will be raw. I'll make certain suggestions to Smith. I'm sure I can get him to where he'll call the officers together. At that meeting we'll make our first move."

"The toxin?"

Tull nodded. "And we will have created the conditions in each of the men for it to work very quickly. We'll take out Smith, the communications officer and the diving officer."

Forbushe indicated he wanted a cigarette. And as Tull held the light for him, he said, "Who do we take out and who does it?"

"Any one of the men," Tull answered, this time releasing the smoke from his mouth. "As to who does it and how it's done, well—leave that to me."

"You're not going to do it, are you?"

Tull shook his head. Then he said, "I want you to make a small bomb. Just powerful enough to blow a chopper out of the air. Have it timed to go off five minutes after the timer is set."

Forbushe nodded.

"You did one hell of a job," Tull said, putting his hand on Forbushe's shoulder. "It won't be hard once we have control of the boat."

51

"How will you get the bomb aboard the chopper?" Forbushe asked.

"In the body bag," Tull said, removing his hand from Forbushe's shoulder. "I want the smallest possible package, understand?"

Nodding, Forbushe stood up. "You'll have it, about the size of a cigarette pack."

"Once the skipper and the other officers are ill, I'll be in command and it will be my recommendation that we abandon our role in the exercises and return immediately to Norfolk. Under the circumstances, with Hasse also on the verge of death, I don't think Gromly will voice any objections."

"I just hope you're right."

Tull nodded. "I know I am. I'm getting paid to be right."

Without answering, Forbushe stubbed out his cigarette and left.

5

Tull was in his bunk, hands behind his head, hovering between wakefulness and sleep. He'd been in a deep, restful sleep for almost an hour and now his inner clock had just about awakened him. He resisted its pull and clung to the dream image of the nude woman, who offered him the nipples on her breasts to suck. Then suddenly a brazen voice filled his brain. "Mister Tull, report to the captain's cabin immediately . . . Mister Tull, report to the captain's cabin immediately."

Tull was wide awake. He'd been called over the 1MC. Picking up the phone alongside his bunk, he punched out the phone number of the captain's cabin.

Smith answered.

"I'm on my way, Captain," Tull said. He stood up, stretched, went to the metal sink jutting out of the opposite bulkhead and turned on the cold water. For an instant, he looked at his reflection in the metal mirror just above the sink. There was stubble on his chin. He rubbed his hand across the rough surface. He decided that he'd grow a beard when he finally turned in his papers. He really disliked shaving. Then for an instant, for absolutely no apparent reason, he had a fleeting memory of his dream. "Bet she'd have offered me a hell of a lot more than the nipples on her tits," he said to his reflection; then, smiling, he doused his face in cold water. Minutes later, he knocked softly on Smith's cabin door.

"Come," Smith called out.

Tull entered the cabin. Gromly and Hasse were already there.

"Sit down, Commander," Smith said, pointing to the only vacant chair in the room.

Tull nodded, looked at Gromly and Hasse and nodded again.

"One of the admiral's men has been murdered," Smith said.

Tull started out of his chair and, checking his movement, dropped back into it again.

"The body was found in the flaghead by Admiral Gromly," Smith continued.

Tull glanced quickly at Gromly. The man was very pale.

"His cock was cut off and stuffed in his mouth," Hasse said, his feeling of revulsion obvious in his tone and the expression on his rugged-looking face.

Tull swallowed hard. "Was that the way he was killed?" he asked, his eyes still on the general.

"Knifed in the back," Gromly said, the words exploding out of him.

Tull uttered a ragged sigh.

"I've radioed for a chopper to take the body off and notified COMSUBLANT of the situation."

"May I smoke, sir?" Tull asked.

Smith nodded. "I requested permission to continue our shakedown cruise and participation in the exercise. Admiral Gromly and General Hasse endorsed both my requests."

"How many of the crew know about the murder?" Tull asked.

"I imagine by now it's all over the boat," Smith said and, shaking his head, he added, "It's impossible to keep something like that quiet."

Tull released smoke through his nose. "Then they know about the cutting off of the man's genitals?" he questioned.

"Sure they know," Hasse answered.

"It's going to make jittery—"

"Scared is more like it." Gromly said, the words exploding out of him again. "Scared shitless to know that there's a killer on board."

"Who was the officer?" Tull questioned.

"Lieutenant John Rider, a communications specialist," Gromly responded.

Tull took a deep drag on the cigarette and blew the smoke up toward the low ceiling. "Sir," he said, looking at the admiral, "I mean no disrespect toward the deceased, but is there the remotest possibility that he had—" Tull hesitated.

"If you're alluding, Commander, to what I think you are, the answer is absolutely no and I mean absolutely no. The man had a reputation for being something of a stud."

Tull nodded. "With all due respect, sir, a reputation for being one thing, especially for being a stud, doesn't, according to the experts on such things, rule out being something else."

Gromly's cheeks turned red.

"Sir, it was only a suggestion for a possible motive," Tull said.

"We'll let the authorities deal with that," Gromly responded testily.

"Yes, sir," Tull answered.

Smith cleared his throat. "John," he said, using Tull's given name, "I want you to personally take charge of putting the body aboard the chopper and I want it done as expeditiously as possible."

"I'll see to it, sir," Tull answered, aware that it was the first time that Smith used his given name.

"The chopper is due here—" Smith looked at his watch "—a half hour, at twenty one thirty. We'll turn on our topside lights. The chopper will take the body aboard by winch."

Tull reached over to Smith's desk and stubbed out his cigarette in an ashtray made from the rear end of a five-inch shell casing. "Where is the body now?" he asked.

"Under guard in the flag wardroom," Gromly responded.

"See the boat's master chief—he knows where the body bags are located," Smith said.

"Yes, sir."

There was a moment of silence, during which Hasse shifted his position and Gromly ran his hand through his thinning hair.

"If there's nothing else, sir," Tull said, "I'll get the detail moving."

"That's all, John," Smith said gravely.

Tull stood up, faced Gromly and Hasse. "Sirs," he said, saluting them.

Each one returned the courtesy.

Tull saluted Smith, and as the salute was returned, he did a precise about-face and headed for the door. Moments later he was out of the captain's cabin and on his way to Forbushe. He'd just given a stellar performance and there was no one present who appreciated it . . .

Forbushe was at his station in the engineering division. He'd already heard about the killing.

"Step outside, Mister Forbushe," Tull said.

"We're doing twenty-eight knots," he said, nodding; then he turned over the watch to one of the junior officers on duty. "Everything is green . . . I'll be back in five minutes."

"Aye, aye, sir," the man answered, taking the place behind the desk vacated by Forbushe.

Tull led the way, and once they were in the passageway, some distance from Forbushe's office, he said, "I need the bomb now."

"It's in my cabin," Forbushe answered.

The two of them walked a short distance toward the stern of the boat to Forbushe's quarters.

"Why the hell did you have to have the man's cock cut off and stuffed in his mouth?" Forbushe asked in a whisper as soon as they were inside his cabin.

"If you don't know, I'm sure as hell not going to take the time now to tell you," Tull answered.

57

Forbushe opened his locker, reached inside and came out with a small metal can slightly smaller than a cigarette pack. "This will do what you want. It has only one setting. Move this gizmo up and in three minutes—well, its powerful enough to blow a good-size hole in the boat."

Tull slipped the bomb in his pocket.

"How are you going to get it in the body bag?" Forbushe asked.

Tull smiled. "I'm in charge of the detail responsible for getting the body aboard the chopper." He headed for the door. "Everything is going our way . . . See you." He was out in the passageway and, almost at a run, headed for the crew's quarters, where he'd pick up his detail. Of course, the four men he'd pick had identified themselves to him with their pieces of the puzzle. He had already used one of them to do the killing and now he'd help get rid of the body.

"Atten'hut!" one of the men called the moment Tull entered the crew's quarters.

"As you were, men," Tull told them. "The following four men come with me: Haines, Moussarakis, Berger and Sansone."

The four men stopped what they were doing and followed Tull out into the passageway.

"Haines, find the master chief and get a body bag from him," Tull said.

"Aye, aye, sir," Haines answered. He was a dark-complexioned man, with a small black mustache and black eyes. Haines was the knifer and cock cutter.

58

"The rest of you follow me," Tull said, leading them to the flag wardroom.

Each armed with an M-16, two second lieutenants on Hasse's staff stood guard at the door. They recognized Tull and snapped to attention.

"At ease," Tull said. "We're here to remove the body."

"Yes, sir," one of the lieutenants said. "He's all yours."

"Consider yourselves relieved," Tull told them.

"Aye, aye, sir," they responded in unison.

Tull opened the wardroom door, stepped aside and gestured the three men with him inside; then following them, he closed the door after himself.

The body, covered with a sheet, was laid out on one of the two tables.

Tull said, "The body goes topside as soon as we get it into the bag." He pulled back the sheet: the man's cock was still stuffed in his mouth and his chin, neck and white T-shirt were stained with dried blood.

Tull glanced at the men around the table. None of them looked away. None of them frowned or, by a change of expression, showed the slightest bit of sympathy for the dead man. They were hard men: all of them were killers . . .

A knock on the door ended his thinking and, pulling the sheet up over the corpse again, he called, "Come ahead."

Haines opened the door, carrying the body bag slung over his shoulder.

"Set the bag out on the deck," Tull told Haines.

He waited until it was unzipped before he said, "Two men at either end of the body lift it and put it in the bag. Okay, now one of you zip it up, but don't close it all the way."

"Done, sir," Sansone said, standing after having zipped the bag almost closed.

"Two on each end and we'll head up to the deck," Tull said. He led them up through the control room, where men averted their eyes and out on the deck, through the bulkhead door in the sail.

The deck was already illuminated with a harsh white light from the boat's floodlights. Smith, Gromly and Hasse were on the bridge.

"Coming to full stop," Smith said over the 1MC. "Radar has the chopper on the scope. He's five minutes out."

With a wave, Tull acknowledged the captain's words; then to his detail, he said, "Bring the body forward, almost to the bow."

"I hear the chopper," Berger said.

"Coming out of the south," Haines commented.

"Now listen to me," Tull said, "as soon as we get the body in the gurney, the four of you block the view from the bridge; then when I say, 'go,' get back to the sail as quickly as you can." His eyes went from man to man and each responded with a nod.

The boat's engine stopped and she began to lose headway.

The roar of the chopper surrounded them; then suddenly its high intensity spotlight came on, and over its PA system, the pilot said, "Coming in over your bow as soon as you're dead in the water."

The boat continued to slow until it was dead in the water.

"Coming down to twenty-five feet," the chopper pilot said.

The wind caused by the chopper's rotors whipped over the boat's deck and caused the water to splash across the deck.

"Stand by to receive the gurney," the pilot ordered.

Moments later the wire basket came out of the chopper's open side door and started to be winched down, but the wind from the rotors made it swing violently from side to side.

"Moussarakis, Haines, grab ahold of that mother," Tull barked, "or it will knock one of us into the drink."

The men reached up, and as soon as it was close enough to grab, they got hold of it and guided it down on to the deck.

"Get the body into it," Tull said.

The dead man was placed into the gurney and Tull quickly slipped the bomb into the body bag. "Go," he said.

The man ran back toward the sail.

Tull signaled the crewman in the chopper to begin winching the body up; then he started back toward the sail.

"I'm on my way," the chopper pilot said over the PA system and the next instant its high intensity light went out, leaving only its navigation lights visible.

Tull looked up at the bridge.

"Clear the deck," Smith ordered.

The boat's lights were turned off and its screw began to turn in the water. Then suddenly, in the direction of the chopper, there was a tremendous explosion out of which a ball of fire seemed to grow, and then that ball of fire broke into pieces that fell into the sea. The time between the explosion and the vast emptiness of the sky was only a matter of seconds.

The high intensity lights came on again and the C-1 turned toward where the fire ball disintegrated and fell into sea.

Minutes later Tull was on the bridge, alongside Smith. A search mission was under way, though everyone—even those aboard who did not see what had happened but only had heard the explosion— knew that there would not be any survivors and that they'd be lucky to pick up the bodies—that is, if the sharks didn't get to them first . . .

By 0200 nothing was found and Smith called off the search mission and summoned all of the boat's officers to a meeting in the wardroom for a general discussion of the situation. Admiral Gromly and Hasse were present also and in a matter of minutes it became clear that fear was the dominant feeling among the officers and the men.

"Under these circumstances," Keith Howard, the diving officer, said, "I don't see how we could operate effectively. There is no doubt in my mind— and I'm sure I speak for everyone on the C-1—that there is a killer on board."

His view was seconded by another officer, who

said, "The men are talking about the boat being jinxed."

Tull glanced at Forbushe, raised his hand, and when he was recognized by Smith, he stood up and said, "If we go back now, without attempting to do what we were sent out to do, all of us can look forward to reassignment. There's no doubt that there is a killer aboard, but in my opinion—he paused and looked at Admiral Gromly before he continued—the man was killed because he'd made an indecent advance toward another man."

Gromly was on his feet. "I won't have that kind of talk about one of my officers."

"Sir, why would the killer have mutilated the body the way he did if not to indicate that—"

"Sir," Forbushe called out, "Mister Tull has a point."

"I meant no disrespect, sir," Tull said, looking at Gromly. "But the way the man was mutilated suggests that perhaps—"

"Your point is well taken, Commander," General Hasse said. "But if that's so, then the same man must have destroyed the chopper to remove the evidence."

"Sir," Forbushe said, without waiting to be recognized by any of the ranking officers, "that explosion could also have been caused by a mechanical malfunction. There is no way to be sure that it was the work of the murderer. The plain fact is that we'll never know." He sat down.

"We still have several hours before we rendezvous with the Blue Battle Group," Smith said. "I have made a full report of the situation to COM-

SUBLANT and included my statement on my position, which, gentlemen, is to return to our home base as soon as possible and let the authorities begin their investigation. I'm expecting to have an answer from COMSUBLANT before our scheduled rendezvous time, which had to be pushed back one full hour because of the circumstances aboard this boat. I have nothing more to say on the matter. Gentlemen, you are dismissed."

Tull nodded to Forbushe, went to the captain and said, "Whatever COMSUBLANT decides, Skipper, you can count on the men." And in a gesture of friendship, he shook his hand. Out of the corner of his left eye, he watched Forbushe shake the admiral's hand, much to the man's astonishment.

Moments later they met outside the wardroom.

"Done," Tull said with a smile.

"Done," Forbushe echoed, grinning.

"Now let's get several of the other officers."

"Who in particular?"

"Communications . . . your assistant . . . the diving officer and the general."

"What about the enlisted men?"

"Some of them are already feeling sick," Tull answered. "With any luck we'll have the boat in a matter of hours. It must be in our hands before we reach the rendezvous point."

"Absolutely," Forbushe agreed.

When they reached the control room, Tull made a routine check of the radar scope, while Forbushe continued on his way to the engine room.

"Nothing in the air," the radar operator said.

"What about under us?" he asked, stepping over

to where the sonar scope was located.

"A clear sea," the sonar man said, "except for some playful dolphins and very noisy shrimp."

Tull laughed and patted the man on the shoulder. "You'll be listening to a hell of a lot more in a few hours."

"I don't mind the dolphins, sir. I can almost tell one from another by the pitch of his click."

Suddenly the 1MC came on. "Mister Tull, report to the captain's cabin on the double."

"No rest for the weary, as the saying goes," Tull said, and headed back to the captain's cabin. When he arrived there, Smith was sitting behind his desk, leaning forward. He was sweating profusely and shaking uncontrollably.

Looking up at him with bleary eyes and laboring with each word, he said, "You have the con."

"Yes, sir," Tull answered; then to the bewildered steward, he said, "Help me get him into his bunk, then I'll call the doc in here."

"Aye, aye, sir," the young man answered and added, "The captain was fine one minute an' like this the next."

"Happens that way sometimes," Tull commiserated.

They moved Smith to his bunk and Tull switched on the 1MC. "All hands now hear this . . . All hands now hear this . . . This is Commander Tull . . . Captain Smith has suddenly become ill . . . I repeat, Captain Smith has suddenly become ill . . . Lieutenant George Hopkins report to the captain's cabin on the double . . . Doctor Hopkins to the captain's cabin on the double." He switched off the 1MC and smoked a cigarette, while he waited for the doctor and the frantic phone call that he knew would come from the flag bridge.

The phone call came first. The admiral himself was on the line. "You'll keep me apprised of the situation," he said.

"A soon as I know something, sir, I'll let you know," Tull told him.

"To tell the truth I'm feeling a bit queasy myself," Gromly admitted.

"Must be in someway connected to the tension. These last few hours haven't been easy."

A knock at the door brought Tull's attention to it. He nodded to the steward to let him in and said to Gromly, "The doctor is here now, sir. As soon as I know something definite, I'll report to you."

"Yes, do that," Gromly said, his speech already slow.

Tull put the phone down just as the doctor entered. He pointed to the bunk area and followed behind him.

Hopkins nodded. He was a tall, well-built man in his late twenties. Originally from Santa Fe, New Mexico, he had graduated from New York University Medical School and entered the Navy through the NROTC. He volunteered for submarine training and was going to become a specialist in medical problems associated with submariners. This was his first sea assignment.

Submarines didn't have regular doctors on board. The medical needs of the crew had always been taken care of by a well-trained pharmacist mate. But since the *C-1* had flag and field-grade officers on board a medical doctor had been assigned to her.

Hopkins did a preliminary examination, checking Smith's heart, looking in his eyes, ears, nose and throat. Then, frowning, he looked up at Tull and said, "My best guess is that he's allergic to something," he said in a distinct western drawl that years away from his home hadn't diminished.

Tull gave him a questioning look. "To what?"

Hopkins shrugged. "I'd have to run a whole mess of tests to find that out."

"That's not possible here, it it, Doc?" Tull asked, knowing it wasn't.

"Not possible," Hopkins confirmed. "Maybe—"

The phone rang.

Answering it, the steward said, "It's for the doc."

"Lieutenant Hopkins here," he said, and then listened.

As Tull watched his facial expression change, he knew that the call must be about one of the other officers . . . perhaps Gromly?

Hopkins put the phone down. "The admiral has been taken ill with, according to the symptoms his aide had just described to me, the same thing that the captain has."

Tull furrowed his brow and looked grave. "Perhaps," he offered, "it's something like Legionnaires' disease. Maybe it's carried through the boat's ventilation system?"

Hopkins seemed not to have heard him as he once again bent over the captain.

"I'll see that the captain is made as comfortable as possible," Tull said, and then something totally unexpected happened.

Hopkins stood up and, scratching his head, he commented, "The symptoms mimic those of a rattlesnake bite. You get to know them where I grew up."

Tull managed to get off a "You're joking." But he suddenly had a new appreciation for Lieutenant Hopkins and more than a deep concern for what would follow. He did not want to kill a doctor, or a steward, but if he had to, he was prepared to have it done.

"Not all the symptoms, mind you, but some of them," Hopkins said. Taking his medical shoulder bag with him, he walked back into the captain's office. "I suppose no one on board just happens to have a pet rattler that got loose?" He laughed before Tull could answer. "It was a rhetorical question, Commander." Then he looked toward the captain's bunk. "I recommend that he be transferred to a hospital as soon as possible."

"Will the medical facilities aboard a carrier do?" Tull asked.

"Yes. The doctors aboard will be able to run the allergy tests and if the admiral's condition is the same as the captain's, then he too should be transferred."

"That will put an end to the planned maneuvers," Tull said, walking the doctor to the door.

Hopkins shrugged. "I can only give you a medical opinion," he said, opening the door. "I'll be back in a little while to check on the captain."

"I'll be in the control room," Tull said.

"I understand . . . You're now the boat's skipper," he responded and saluted.

Tull returned the salute and, stepping back into the cabin, he told the steward to make the captain as comfortable as possible, "and do not permit anyone near him without my permission and then, to be sure that the person has my permission, phone me. I'll either be in the control room or in my cabin."

"Aye, aye, sir," the steward replied with a salute.

Tull returned the courtesy and headed for the control room. He'd wait to acknowledge the message from COMSUBLANT before ordering the boat to dive and change its course.

6

Detective Guy Markham, NYPD Homicide Division, was on a one-week vacation in Virginia Beach, where he'd met Karin Woods. Karin, a high school art teacher in the town of Falmouth, Kentucky, was also on vacation.

Guy had met Karin on the beach, in front of the Holiday Inn, where the two of them were staying, the afternoon he'd arrived. And in a matter of hours, he had invited her to dinner and, after having danced until after midnight, they wound up in bed, in Guy's room.

Karin was a lovely-looking twenty-four-year-old woman with a frank, open face, decorated with a sprinkling of freckles, some of which spilled down to the tops of her breasts, blue eyes, long red hair and a body that—as the expression went—didn't quit.

And Guy was enjoying every inch of her, including her southern accent, which, for some reason he couldn't understand, made her even more desirable.

Even in the dim light coming from the night table, he could see the sex blush suffuse her face, neck and breasts; even her ears turned red.

"I'm ready," she said, entwining her arms around his neck.

He eased himself into her and, bending low over her face, he kissed her tenderly on the lips and then with increasing passion as he quickened his movements.

She opened her mouth, gave him her tongue and at the same time thrust her hips against him.

Guy liked the taste of her and told her so.

"Faster, go faster," she whispered. "Yes, yes . . . Oh . . . Oh, I'm coming . . . I'm coming." Her body tensed, then seemed to implode and, as she trembled in his embrace, she cried out, "Oh . . . Oh . . . Oh Lord . . . Lord!"

Guy held the sound of her voice in his ears as his own passion roared to a climax and, with a wordless growl of sheer delight, he crushed her to him. "It was good," he said, taking several deep breaths. "Very good!"

For several minutes, they remained wrapped in each other's embrace, and then Guy reached over to the automatic TV control and switched on the set.

"Only news and talk shows on now, honey," Karin said.

"No late-night movies?" Guy asked, pulling himself up to rest against the bed's backboard. He was a man of middling height, somewhat chunky, with well-developed muscles from working out with weights for fifteen minutes every morning. Dark-haired, with gray eyes, he seldom went to bed alone on a Saturday night.

"I don't know the stations down here. Maybe there is one," Karin said, snuggling close to him.

He tried several stations and, settling on a news program, he put his arm around Karin and fondled her breast. "Making love always gives me an appetite," he said as a commercial for Steakums came on.

Karin laughed. "Me too," she admitted.

He looked down at her and squeezed her breast. "Maybe next time we'll get some sandwiches and have them in the room waiting for us."

"Alright."

"Some beer too," Guy said as the commercial left the screen and the camera zoomed in on the newscaster.

"The police still do not have any leads on the man who was murdered last night and then mutilated. We were informed by sources who do not wish to be identified that the victim's genitals were stuffed in his mouth. This is the second killing of an identical nature . . . And now to—"

Guy bolted out of bed.

"What's wrong, honey?" Karin asked.

"That murder the commentator just spoke about—"

"What about it?"

"I had a John Doe just like that a few days before I came down here," he said. "A young guy was found with his cock sliced off and stuffed in his mouth in the West Shore Motel on Staten Island."

"Ugh, that's disgusting!"

"Yeah, sure is," he said, reaching for the telephone.

"Who are you calling?"

"The detective on the case—maybe my purp is down here now," he said and dialed the operator.

"But you're on vacation," she reminded him.

"Doesn't matter," he answered above the phone. "I'm still a cop."

The operator came on.

"Would you connect me to the central police station," he said.

"There is no central police station," she told him. "There's only one station house for the area."

"Alright, would you please connect me to it."

"You can get the number from Information—"

"Operator, this is police business. Now put that call through or let me speak to your supervisor." In a matter of moments, he was speaking to the desk sergeant and after he identified himself, he said, "I want to speak to the detective handling the murder in the motel," he said.

"Lieutenant Charles Benjamin is in charge of the investigation. But he won't be in until tomorrow morning."

"Can I reach him at home?" Guy asked.

"No, sir, it's against the department's rules to release the telephone numbers of its personnel. But you can meet him here at nine o'clock tomorrow morning."

"Leave word that Detective Guy Markham will be in to see him."

"I'll do that, sir . . . Detective, where are you

staying while you're in Virginia Beach."

"The Holiday Inn," Guy answered. "Please make sure he gets my message."

"Will do," the duty sergeant replied.

"Thank you," Guy said, and put the phone down. "I'll see the detective in charge of the investigation in the morning." He looked down at Karin.

Holding the light blanket up, she said, "Come back to bed."

He smiled and, sliding down next to her, he immediately felt the warmth radiating from her naked body; then as they moved together, the warmth fused with a wonderful softness. He began to caress the broad of her back, then the wonderful rotundity of her rump and the deep crevice between; and when the tips of his fingers finally glided over the warm, wet lips of her sex, he felt her hand moving deftly over his shaft.

"This time," she whispered, "let's do it the French way."

"Any way you want, baby," he answered.

Tull took the communique' from COMSUBLANT off the teletype himself before either the communications officer or the rate on duty could do it.

COMSUBLANT left the decision to return up to Smith, acting on advice from Admiral Gromly and General Hasse.

"To COMSUBLANT," he said to the communications officer. "Will proceed as planned . . . You know to whom this is to be sent to," he said.

75

"Vice Admiral George W. Hicks, COM-SUBLANT, Norfolk, Virginia."

"Send it," Tull said with a nod; then returning to the control room, he pressed the klaxon button twice and over the 1MC, he said, "Dive . . . Dive . . . All hands, clear the deck . . . All hands, clear the deck."

The topside watch dropped through the open hatchway and the last man pulled it down and dogged it shut.

"Board green," an officer reported.

"Secure radio mast," Tull said.

"Radio mast secured," the communications officer responded.

"DO, make one hundred and twenty-five feet," Tull ordered.

"Making one hundred and twenty-five feet," Lieutenant Howard responded.

The C-1 dropped quickly through the water.

Tull watched the depth gauge; they were down fifty feet in less than a minute and a half.

"Stand by to activate manual diving controls," the DO said as the C-1 was approaching its depth. The boat settled at 125 feet. "Trimmed to the mark," he called out.

Tull gave him a thumbs-up signal and then made a quick check of the sonar scope.

"More dolphins," the operator told him.

He nodded. There were ten men ill, and from the way the DO and the communications officers looked they would soon make the number twelve. As the key members of the crew became ill, Tull assigned their duties to the various men, who gave him pieces of the puzzle.

The doctor was now among those who were ill. Tull had decided that it would have been too risky to keep him around. He might have taken his guess about the snake venom a couple of steps further and reached the conclusion that, somehow, some kind of venomlike substance had been injected into the men who had fallen ill.

Forbushe came up to the control room and signaled that he wanted to speak to Tull.

"We can't remain on our present heading much longer," he whispered.

Tull nodded. "I plan to change course in thirty minutes."

"We want to get as far away from this area as possible before we turn on our real course."

"I plan to send out a May Day over our low frequency transmitter, with no position given. That should confuse them for a while."

Forbushe looked over at the DCO and the communications officer. "They'll be down soon. We should be in complete operating control of the boat within the hour."

Tull didn't acknowledge the comment. He had the feeling that Forbushe had something else he wanted to say, but held himself back.

"From now on," Forbushe said, "I will be in the control room with you."

Tull almost smiled. He was right: Forbushe did have something else to say.

"You agree with that, don't you?" Forbushe asked.

"I agree with it," Tull answered, realizing that if he

didn't, Forbushe would sulk and become difficult and, with everything going so smoothly, it would be foolish on his part to create one difficulty that might quickly lead to several others.

Forbushe looked satisfied and said, "I'll be back when you change course."

"Good idea," Tull told him, and as he turned away from Forbushe, he saw the DCO suddenly drop to the deck and then the communications officer went down. For all practical purposes, the *C-1* was completely under his command . . .

Detective Lieutenant Charles Benjamin arrived at the police station at 8:30 in the morning. Despite the fact he'd heard the DJ on the local Golden Oldies radio show announce, while driving from his house on the beach in Norfolk, that the eight o'clock temperature outside the studio had already reached ninety, he carried a container of hot black coffee and a whole wheat doughnut in a white paper bag. He'd stopped, as he did every morning, at the County Doughnut store where he had his first cup of black coffee for the day and his first whole wheat doughnut of the morning before he'd ordered the container of coffee and a second whole wheat doughnut to go.

Benjamin's desk was in a multi-hued, multi-paneled cubicle, with a view past one of the panels of the window on the other side of the office, which was, according to his body thermostat, too cold in the summer and too damn hot in the winter. He set the bag down on the desk before he removed his jacket and, carefully draping it on a hanger, hung it in the metal locker behind his desk chair. He sat down, opened the bag, removed the container of coffee, the doughnut and two napkins from the bag; then he flattened the bag out on the desk to serve as a coaster for the container and someplace to put the doughnut. Picking up the phone he asked the day desk sergeant if there were any messages for him.

"Some guy from the NYPD. Says he has a lead on that motel killing," the desk sergeant said.

"When?"

"When what?"

"When the fuck will he be here?" Benjamin growled.

"Sometime today, I guess," the desk sergeant answered.

Benjamin slammed the phone down. This fucking day was starting out to be like the several thousand he'd already experienced. He opened the V in the top of the container's plastic top, lifted the container and began to drink. The laid-back attitude—his own included from time to time—never ceased to amaze him. The fucking message was a case in point. The night desk sergeant didn't even bother to put down the caller's name, or get the time—

The phone rang.

"Lieutenant Benjamin here," he answered.

"That guy from the NYPD is here," the desk sergeant said.

"Thanks, I'll be out to get him," Benjamin said, and put the container of coffee down. For a moment, he considered slipping into his jacket, but gave up the idea and, with a shrug, walked out of the squad room.

A cop can always spot another cop, so the old saw went, and this was no exception. This one wore a pair of gray slacks, a blue polo shirt and a pair of those expensive sneakers. He was dark complexioned and his bare arms rippled muscles. Benjamin was almost certain the guy was wearing a snub nose .38 on his right leg. But it was his eyes that gave him away, made the difference between him and other men. Cops, reporters and some novelists have the same kind of eyes—not nervous, but moving to take it all in, to see what most people don't even know is there . . .

"Lieutenant Benjamin," he said, extending his hand.

"Guy Markham," the man answered, vigorously pumping Benjamin's hand. "So you got my message."

"Yeah, I got it," Benjamin said, casting a withering look at the desk sergeant, who responded with a slight smile and a grin. He let go of Markham's hand and began walking back toward the squad room.

Markham followed.

When they reached Benjamin's desk, he said, "Pull up a chair and I'll share my coffee and doughnut with you." He opened the side drawer and took out a chipped white mug. I take mine black."

"Black is fine."

Benjamin stopped pouring when the mug was half filled and pushed it toward his guest; then he snapped the doughnut into approximately equal

80

portions and, pointing to one of them, he said, "It's not much, but it is a sign of hospitality."

Nodding, Markham agreed, drank some of the hot black coffee and said, "I have a John Doe in Staten Island just like the three you have here."

Before Benjamin could answer, another detective, with a balding head, poked his face around a yellow panel and asked, "Did you hear about that car blowing up last night on sixty?"

Benjamin screwed his eyes up at the man. "I've got my own problems, Lou. I don't need someone else's."

"The car was rigged with a time bomb," Lou said.

'So?"

"There wasn't much to ID the guy driving, but the VIN was intact. The car was rented from a local place called Big Al's by a Commander John Tull."

"So the driver was ID'd," Benjamin commented.

Lou shook his head. "Commander Tull, according to the Navy, is aboard a submarine."

"Then who the hell was blown up?"

"We're working on it," Lou answered. "But here's something else, someone, maybe the commander, tried to take the VIN off with acid, but enough of the last four digits were left to trace."

"When you get something connected to my dead John Does, come see me," Benjamin said.

"Just making morning conversation," Lou said, smiling at Guy. "He's not a purp, is he?"

"He's with the NYPD," Benjamin said. "Detective Guy Markham, Detective Louis Walker.

Markham started to stand.

"Stay put," Walker said, waving to him. "Chuck

can use all the help you, or anyone else, can give him."

Markham grinned.

"Get your face out of my cubicle or I'll throw something at it," Benjamin said.

Winking broadly at Markham, Lou said, "Just trying to help, Chuck, just trying to help." And he disappeared behind the panel.

"There are guys like that in every squad room," Markham said. "I sometimes think if we didn't have them, a lot more of us would go off the deep end."

Benjamin looked at his guest with new interest. He didn't expect much from a muscle man and certainly nothing as profound an insight as he'd just verbalized. "Tell me about your John Doe," he said, taking a sip of coffee.

"Same as your three . . . dead with his shlong stuffed in his mouth. He was found by a maid in the West Shore Motel."

Benjamin bit into his half of the doughnut. "Just to play this out by the book, do you have any ID to show me?"

Markham produced his gold shield and ID card. "Call seven one eight seven twenty, twenty one twenty and ask to speak to Captain Richard Monty, he's my boss."

"These are good enough," Benjamin said, handing the shield and plastic ID card back to his guest.

"I heard about your John Does on the late news last night," Markham explained as he pocketed his two pieces of ID.

"On vacation here?" Benjamin asked.

"A week."

"Come down with a friend?"

"No, but—"

Holding up his hand, Benjamin said, "I get the picture . . . You get anything back on the guy's prints?"

Markham shook his head. "The Agency is slow getting a make on John Does. Not really a very high priority."

Benjamin nodded his agreement. "I haven't got the first two back either." He finished eating the doughnut, drank the rest of the coffee and dropped the container into the wastepaper basket. "It's the same MO," he said, putting the white paper bag into the basket. "But that might be the result of one crazy doing what another crazy had already done."

"Possibility . . . but there's also another possibility," Markham answered.

"I'm listening."

"The four stiffs could be the result of one crazy."

Benjamin cupped one hand at the side of the desk and, with one of the napkins, he brushed the doughnut crumbs into his cupped palm, emptying it into the wastepaper basket. "They could be. But if they were, did they have something in common, or were they just at the wrong place at the wrong time?"

"The way they were done smacks of something sexual."

"Yeah, that's for sure."

"Maybe the purp moved from place to place," Markham suggested, finishing his coffee and doughnut.

"Place to place, you think?"

"It's worth a few phone calls to, maybe Boston,

Chicago, St. Louis—"

"Frisco, San Diego, Seattle and, say, Denver."

"Something just might come up."

"You take the cities you named, I'll take the others," Benjamin said. "Use the phone on any unoccupied desk. Tell the switchboard operator you're making the calls for me."

"Okay," Markham responded as he stood up and then, remembering how neat Benjamin was, he took a moment to sweep the doughnut crumbs on the desk in front of him into his hand and then dump them in the wastebasket. "This needs to be washed," he said, starting to pick up the coffee mug.

"Leave it, I'll take care of it later . . . Make those calls."

"I'm on my way," Markham responded, leaving the cubicle.

7

Captain Peter Randle, Assistant Chief of Operations to Vice Admiral George W. Hicks, read the message with an expression of dismay filling his face. His green eyes narrowed and his black beetle brows arched as he looked up at the orderly and asked, "Has anyone else other than the man who copied this seen it?" He was fierce-looking, with a hawklike face, made fiercer looking by his bushy eyebrows that were joined together by a bridge of black hair.

"The watch officer, Commander Robert Hallway," the yeoman answered. "As soon as it came in, he had me bring it to you."

"Pass the word to the watch officer that any message concerning *Command One* is to be treated as 'top secret,'" Randle ordered.

"Aye, aye, sir," the man answered.

"Dismissed," Randle said.

The man saluted and Randle returned the salute; then, picking up the phone, he dialed the number for

Admiral Hicks's red phone.

Before the first ring was completed, the admiral answered.

"Sir, I've just received word that *Command One* has sent a May Day," he said.

Except for the sound of the admiral's ragged breathing, he was absolutely silent.

"No position was given," Randle said.

Finally the admiral asked, "Is she still sending?"

"Negative. Just one transmission via the ELF system."

"My office immediately," Hicks said.

"Yes, sir," Randle responded and, putting the phone down, he headed for the door.

It took until one o'clock in the afternoon for Markham and Benjamin to finish making their calls and, when they did, they sat down at Benjamin's desk and smiled at each other.

"One in Boston and one in Chicago," Markham said.

"Two in Seattle, one in San Diego and two in Frisco. Your one and my three makes four, the two you located makes six, and with those I found we have a total of ten across the country with the same MO and committed at different times."

"Any of yours have a make on their prints?" Markham asked.

"None."

"None of mine either," Markham said.

Benjamin leaned back in his swivel chair, looked at his watch and said, "Let's grab a bite of lunch and

86

think this thing through, unless you've made other plans?"

"Lunch it is, but first I'd like to use the phone."

Benjamin pushed the phone over to the side of the desk near his guest. "Private?" he asked.

Markham nodded.

"When you're finished, meet me in the lobby," Benjamin said, leaving the desk and taking his coat out of the locker.

In a matter of minutes, the phone in Markham's room was ringing. It rang four times before Karin answered it.

"It's Guy," he said.

"I thought you'd be back here by now," she said, "so that we could spend the afternoon on the beach together."

"Something has come up," he answered. "I'll be there as soon as I can. I'll check the beach as soon as I get back."

She started to say something, but he said, "Last night was great, hon. See you later." He hung up and as he went to meet Benjamin in the lobby, he suddenly realized that he was being unfair to Karin. She couldn't help but think that, as far as he was concerned, all she was good for was a roll in the sack. He realized he didn't want her to think that and decided to make it up to her, when he saw her later in the day.

A few minutes later, Benjamin and Markham

were seated opposite each other at a table in Wendy's, a five-minute drive from the police station. The place was noisy, crowded with lunchtime clientele.

Benjamin was involved with a cheeseburger and Markham was having various veggies from the salad bar.

"I eat here because it's convenient," Benjamin said. "Sometimes I even come back for dinner." He managed a smile. "You know how it is being a bachelor. There are just some nights I don't feel like cooking, and I'm a damn good cook."

"I figured you to be married," Markham commented.

"Was, until a year ago," Benjamin responded, picking up a couple of thin fries with his fingers. "It just didn't work anymore. Know what I mean, when I say that it 'didn't work out anymore'?"

"I had the same thing happen with a woman I. lived with for a couple of years," Markham responded.

"Alright, let's get down to what we have," Benjamin told him.

"Spell it out."

"We got ten guys stiffed in different places at different times and all with the same MO," Benjamin said, finishing off the last piece of the cheeseburger. "In my book that gives more questions than we had before."

"There's got to be a connection somewhere."

"Different cities, different guys."

"Any connection between the cities?"

"Most of them are located on the Coast, okay."

"Chicago isn't," Markham said.

"Anything else?" Benjamin asked.

"All of the stiffs are young, probably in their early twenties."

"The crazy or crazies had a thing for young guys," Benjamin said. "Most of those kind do."

"If we could get the Bureau to shake ass on at least one set of prints, we might have something," Markham commented. "But they move at their own pace, in their own fucking world."

Benjamin smiled. The more time he spent with this NYPD cop, the more he liked him. In many ways, he reminded him of himself years ago, when he was full of fire for the job. "I tell you what," he said, "you go back to your lady friend at the motel and if something breaks, I'll give you a ring."

Markham ignored the suggestion. "Don't you know anyone who can get a make on the prints at the Bureau?"

Benjamin shook his head.

Suddenly Markham frowned and leaned toward the table across the aisle, where two young women were seated. "Excuse me," he said, "I couldn't help overhearing what you were talking about. Are you sure that one of our submarines went down?"

Benjamin had noticed them as soon as they sat down. Both were young, somewhere in their early thirties. Both were married; the telltale ring was on each of their third fingers, left hand. One was slightly taller than the other. Both had brown hair, but the shorter of the two wore hers longer. They looked sad. The taller one's eyes were red.

The two of them nodded, almost in unison, then

the shorter one said, "My neighbor's husband is the sonar officer on board. Lily, that's her name, was notified a short time ago."

"It was announced over the radio as we were driving here," the other woman said.

"Did the announcer happen to mention the submarine's name and number?"

"No," the first woman who spoke answered, "but Lily told me that her husband, Howard, was on a special kind of a submarine. I think it was called *Command One*."

"Thank you," Markham said, repositioning himself at his table. "I put four years in aboard a sub."

Benjamin nodded sympathetically.

"I might even know some of the guys on board," Markham commented, his voice low with obvious concern.

"Go back to the motel," Benjamin said gently, aware of the anguish reflected in the man's eyes. The light had suddenly dulled in them. "I promise, I'll call if something comes up. Cm'on I'll drive you."

Vice Admiral Hicks was meeting with his staff in the conference room at COMSUBLANT headquarters. A short, wiry man of sixty, he was built more like a fighter pilot than a submariner. Seated at the head of a huge, highly polished oak wood table, he said, "I don't want any word to get to the press about the murder, or the subsequent loss of the chopper. News about the chopper can be delayed for at least another twenty-four to forty-eight hours. And when we do release information to the press, it must be done in a way to make it seem that the chopper was lost while searching for the *C-1*. Is that understood?"

The men at the table nodded.

Then Randle, who had been on the phone at the opposite side of the room, put the phone down and took his place to the right of Hicks. "Sir," he said, "the President wants to know why we haven't initiated any rescue operation."

Hicks closed his eyes, opened them and said, "I already explained to the Secretary of the Navy that we did not have a fix on the *C-1* and that she is down in at least ten thousand feet of water, perhaps even fifteen. I had hoped that he would have explained the situation to the President. There is nothing we can do. We probably won't even be able to locate the wreckage." Then he added, "I should have ordered her immediate return after the problem she encountered on her first deep dive."

"Our intelligence people are looking into the possibility of sabotage," a staff member said. "From Captain's Smith report on the deep-dive incident and the destruction of the chopper, well—sabotage is a possibility."

"I'd have to agree," Hicks replied.

"I took the liberty of having the families of each of the members of the crew notified, if they live in the area, by an officer going directly to the individual's home, and if the man lives out of the area, informing the family by phone," Randle said. "In either the home visit or the notification by phone, the family was told that the man was listed as missing."

"Yes, that was the way to do it," Hicks responded;

then with a deep sigh, he added, "Going down in those depths—" He couldn't finish what he'd started to say and after a moment, he said, "There's nothing else we can do, except, if we're praying men, to pray that somehow the disaster did not happen. That's all gentlemen, for now. Dismissed."

Tull ordered the *C-1* to a depth of one thousand feet and came to a new course that would bring the boat into the South Atlantic.

"She's making forty knots," Forbushe said, "and probably can do fifty."

Tull checked the sonar scope. Haines was manning it.

"All clear," Haines reported.

"We have the entire crew under guard of lock and key," Forbushe said. "But all of them are too sick now to give us any trouble."

Tull went to the navigation computer. "I intend to make a run south for a thousand miles, then do a one-eighty and head straight for the toll booth. Once we're through, our friends will be there to greet us."

"Given our present speed that run south will take us approximately twenty-four hours," Forbushe said.

"Give and take about an hour."

"The run up to the slot will take another twenty-four, possibly longer if we have to take any evasive actions."

"You can count on having to take evasive actions," Tull said. "Sooner or later, we'll be spotted and ID'd."

92

Forbushe agreed. "But we could probably outrun anything on or below the sea."

"That's what I'm counting on," Tull answered.

"Where exactly will our friends be waiting for us?"

"Just past the toll gate. We'll be in Russian waters and out of reach of American ships, or any of her NATO friends."

Forbushe nodded, but didn't say anything.

8

Markham rested against the bed's backboard and stared at the six o'clock news. Karin was alongside him. The two of them were naked. He'd tried to make love to her, but couldn't. Karin had been very understanding about it.

"And now," the announcer said, "in what is being called the worst submarine disaster since the *Thresher* went down off the coast of Cape Cod, the Navy has said that *Command One* was on a routine shakedown cruise after having been refitted. The submarine commanded by Captain Donald Smith was based here in Norfolk. In an off-camera interview with Vice Admiral Hicks our reporter was told that the *Command One* was refitted to serve as a command operations center for various kinds of military operations. He also said that a rescue operation would be impossible and fruitless at the depth where the submarine is thought to have gone down.

"Just before airtime the authorities released a list

of the men on board the downed submarine. Many of them are from this area."

The voice stopped, Taps was softly played, and one by one the name and photograph of each member of the crew was on the screen for several seconds.

"Do you know any of them?" Karin questioned in a whisper.

Markham shook his head but didn't answer. More faces and names moved across the screen; then suddenly a face and name came on that brought a frown to Markham's face. He moved to the foot of the bed to get a closer look at the sailor's face. "That guy looks familiar," he said.

"Karl Fisher," Karin said, reading the name off the screen.

Another photograph and name came into view on the screen.

Markham moved back to the headboard.

"Were you on the same submarine?" Karin asked.

"I'm not sure. I mean, the face is familiar, but—"

"That sometimes happens to me," she said, snuggling close to him. "The face seems so familiar, but I can't connect it to a name. There's supposed to be at least one double for each of us, someone who looks exactly the way you do, or the way I do."

He glanced down at her. One of her nipples was against his chest, the other was visible. He put his arm around her and said, "Listen, I know this whole thing must seem real weird to you, but—"

She put her finger over his lips. "I like you," she said. "I like you because you're gentle and I like you because you care about what you're doing. You

96

don't have to explain anything to me."

"I like you too, Karin," he answered. "And not just because we've made it. It was great last night, by the way."

"For me too," Karin said.

He kissed her passionately on her lips and at the same time gently caressed her breasts.

"Make love to me, Guy," she said.

He eased her down and kissed her neck, her breasts, the hollow of her stomach and then the moist lips of her sex, while she moaned with pleasure.

They moved, allowing her to use her tongue and lips on his penis. He shuddered with delight and then they faced each other and she placed his shaft inside her.

For several moments, neither one of them moved.

"You feel good inside me," Karin said.

Brushing her erect nipples with the tips of his fingers, he began to move.

Karin closed her eyes.

He put his lips to hers.

"Faster," she whispered.

He moved his hand over her nates and along the crack between them.

"It's good with you," she gasped. "It's really good with you!"

He moved faster.

She clutched at his shoulder and made low, throaty sounds.

He could feel her nails move across his back.

"Oh, Guy," she cried. "Guy, I'm there!" And she raked his bare shoulder.

The very next instant he closed his eyes and, with a wordless exclamation of pleasure, he exploded into her. "Wonderful," he gasped. "You're a wonderful woman." And he pressed his face between her soft warm breasts.

Several minutes later, they separated.

"Hungry?" Karin asked.

"Starved," he answered.

Suddenly the phone rang.

Karin looked questioningly at him.

"It's either from New York, or Lieutenant Benjamin," he said, reaching over and picking up the phone.

Benjamin was on the other end. "Have you seen the news on TV?" he asked.

"Yes. The six o'clock."

"Did you see the names and photographs—"

"Yes," Markham said, pulling himself up into a sitting position.

"Three of those guys are my stiffs," Benjamin said. "Can you get your ass down here?"

Suddenly Markham made the connection: his John Doe was Karl Fisher.

"Are you still on?" Benjamin asked.

"I'm here," Markham said.

"Can you make it down here?"

Markham glanced at Karin. "Yeah, I'll be there."

"I'll send a squad car for you. See you," Benjamin said.

Markham put the phone down. "There's a make on three—four of the John Does. Three of them are in the morgue here and one is in the morgue in Staten Island, that's if he hasn't been moved to

98

Bellevue." He began to dress.

Karin sat up. "You mean that man, Karl Fisher, was killed in New York?"

"In a motel on Staten Island," Markham answered, slipping on his polo shirt.

"But how could they be on the submarine and—"

"Honey, I don't know how," he said, pulling up his right trouser leg to strap on the leg holster.

"When will you be back?" Karin asked.

He bent over her and ran his hands through her hair and across her bare breasts. "I might be falling in love with you," he said before he kissed her.

"I think I'd like that," she responded.

Markham smiled. "So would I," he said. He kissed her again, gently squeezed each of her breasts and went to the door. Just as he stepped out of the lobby, a squad car pulled up.

The uniform rolled the window down. "You the NYPD detective?"

Markham nodded.

"Front or back?" the man asked.

"Front," Markham said.

Moments later, he was seated next to the uniform and, with siren screaming and roof lights flashing, they raced through the streets.

Benjamin was at his desk with a half dozen eight-by-tens of the dead men on his desk when Markham joined him. "Got the Bureau's report back on the first John Doe, whose real name is Vincent Fields, Chief Petty Officer, radar specialist. The photographs match and so do the prints." He laid out a photograph of the dead man and the one shown on the TV station.

Markham nodded. "I'll call my command and have them fax a copy of Fisher's photograph here."

"This is the Bureau's print report," Benjamin said with satisfaction.

"What the hell is going on with this?" Markham questioned.

"Well, for openers, my guess is that all of the men—the ten of them—were killed in order to put ten other men on that submarine. I checked with the Bureau and was told to call Naval Intelligence. I should be getting a call from them any minute. In the meantime, I've requested photos of the six other John Does. They're being faxed here now."

Markham sat down. "Ten men replaced by ten other men and the submarine down in water so deep, it can't even be reached. I still want to know what the hell is going on." He looked across the desk at Benjamin.

"Listen, we ID'd the men. Now it's up to the Navy to come up with all of the other answers."

Markham ran his hand over his chin. "I hate to say this, but maybe it was a good thing that the submarine went down."

Benjamin reached into the top drawer and pulled out a cigar, removed the cellophane wrapper, rolled the cigar between his thumb and forefinger and, smelling it, he said, "I guess you're right. One thing is for sure, the Navy brass are off the hook. It's a mystery everyone can speculate about." He cut one end of the cigar and put it in his mouth. "I only smoke cigars on special occasions and I consider this a special occasion . . . so special that I'm going to offer you a cigar and together we can happily asphyxiate everyone else in the squad room."

"I don't smoke," Markham answered.

"I should have known that anyone who eats a salad when he could eat a greasy hamburger wouldn't smoke."

Markham grinned. "You're really feeling good!"

Benjamin took the cigar out of his mouth and said, "You should too."

"I do."

"Good," Benjamin said and put the cigar back in his mouth. "I didn't interrupt anything when I called, did I? I mean, anything going on between you and your lady friend? Because if I did, I'm sorry."

"You know, you're a dirty old man."

Benjamin laughed. "So what's wrong with that?"

The phone rang before Markham could respond.

Benjamin picked up the phone and identified himself.

"I'm Captain Jededeah Pilcher, Naval Intelligence," he said. "I understand you have some information that you think might be of interest to us." He had a deep base voice.

Benjamin signaled Markham to pick up a phone. "Detective Markham is picking up an extension," he explained.

"I'm on," Markham said.

"Captain, I have positively ID'd four John Does who are listed as missing aboard the submarine *Command One*," Benjamin said, with the cigar still in his mouth.

Pilcher was absolutely silent.

"There are six others that I am certain will be ID'd," Benjamin told him before he took the cigar out of his mouth and put it down on half a clam shell that served as an ashtray.

"I don't understand what you're talking about," Pilcher said. "How could you ID our men?"

"Three of the men were killed here. You may have read about it."

"Yes, I did. Gruesome murders."

"Identical murders were committed in New York, Frisco, San Diego and Seattle, making a total of ten. All of them were John Does . . . that means no ID."

"I know that!" The note of irritation in Pilcher's voice was obvious.

"All of them were members of the *Command One*'s crew," Benjamin said.

"That's impossible. Her crew was complete when she sailed."

"The total number of men was correct," Benjamin explained. "But ten men who were supposed to be on board weren't; they'd been replaced by ten others. I have the photos and prints to prove it."

"You're telling me that there were ten impostors aboard that submarine and that to put them there, ten crew men were murdered?"

"That's exactly what I'm telling you, Captain," Benjamin answered.

Again there was a silence of several moments before Pilcher said, "You better come here and we'll go into this matter further. Come into the base through Gate Three, identify yourself to the Marine guard, and you and your colleague will be escorted to our building. In the meantime you're not to discuss this with anyone, including your superiors."

"Yes, sir," Benjamin snapped, then added, "But if memory serves me correctly, you don't have any authority to tell me with whom I may or may not discuss my findings."

"Alright, I get the point," Pilcher said. "I did not mean to make my request sound like an order."

"That's what it sounded like to me. What about you, Markham, did it sound like an order to you?"

"I'm asking you not to discuss your findings with anyone, at least until we can evaluate what is going on."

"You got it," Benjamin said. "I'll see you in a half hour. Tell your Marine guard we'll be in a squad car. That way he can't miss us."

"I'll tell him," Pilcher said.

The line went dead.

Benjamin put the phone down and picked up his cigar. "Don't much care to be ordered to do anything," he said when Markham returned.

"You bent his nose."

"Yeah, I guess I did," Benjamin said, "and I enjoyed doing it."

"You know, it's still a police problem. We don't have any idea who did it, or why?"

"You're wrong," Benjamin said, blowing smoke to his left, "we have one *why:* the reason for killing the men was to put ten different men on the submarine. We don't know the other *why:* why did someone want to put ten different men on the submarine, and of course we don't know anything about the *who's*—who was behind it and who did

103

the killing?"

"Now with the submarine down, there's no way we're going to find out any of those answers," Markham commented.

Gathering up the photographs and fingerprint reports from the FBI, Benjamin put each in a separate manila folder and then placed the folders in a large eleven-by-fourteen envelope. "I'm ready to go meet the Navy, what about you?"

"Ready," Markham answered.

9

"It's amazing," Haines said, "that this boat can be operated with only a dozen men, counting you and Forbushe."

Tull nodded. He and Haines were in the ward-room having a coffee and a sandwich. "But it doesn't leave much leeway," Tull responded. "By the time we're done, all of us will be very tired men and sick of eating sandwiches."

"Moussarakis is a damn good cook," Haines said. "He doesn't like to mention it. But I was with him before and he cooked some damn good dishes, using whatever we could kill. He might want to do it."

"I'll talk to him . . . Where were the two of you?" Tull asked. He knew nothing about any of the men. They were chosen by others. He hadn't even known Forbushe until he'd reported aboard the *C-1*.

"East Africa," Haines said, his pale blue eyes peering at Tull over the white rim of the coffee mug. He was a six-footer with close-cropped brown hair, a deceptively innocent-looking face and easy manner about him. "Ever been there?" he asked, lowering the mug.

"Not my beat. But I've been in other places. The Lebanon. A couple of trips back in country," he said, using the accepted expression for having fought in Vietnam.

Haines gave a low whistle, but didn't say anything.

"And some work in various parts of Europe."

"That's white-glove stuff. Done a bit of it myself."

Tull stood up. "I'm going to sack out for a half hour," he said, "but first I'm going to talk to Moussarakis about doing some cooking for us."

Haines got to his feet too. "How long before we're off this boat?" he asked.

"With luck ninety-six hours," Tull said. "That's if we make it straight through without any interference."

"What's our chances for doing that?"

"Let me answer this way, I wouldn't count on it. There's a clock ticking and with every tick that happens, we get closer to the wire. If we have more luck than brains, we'll be able to slip under that wire. But if not—well, then all of us will have been underpaid, no matter how much we signed for."

"Yeah, I figured it would probably turn out to be something like that."

"There's no sense sweating it, though," Tull said, moving to the door, "at least not now."

Haines grinned. "I don't sweat things like that. That's not my style."

"I didn't think it was."

"Forbushe, now there's a man who's a sweater."

"There's always someone who is," Tull responded, finding it strange that Haines should have made that comment about Forbushe to him. Haines, like all of the men, wasn't much of a talker and yet during the last few minutes, he'd said a great deal.

"I'm going to sack out for a while too," Haines said, following Tull out into the passageway and turning toward the crew's quarters.

"See you the next watch," Tull called after him; then, heading for the reactor compartment, where Moussarakis was on duty, he was still thinking about Haines, when he suddenly realized that by mentioning Moussarakis as a possible cook, Haines had given him the name of another man, who he could count on in a tight situation. The fact that the man could cook was serendipitous to the situation. But then Tull found himself faced with two questions: in what situation would he have to rely specifically on them, and did they know something that he didn't?

There wasn't any way he could answer either one of those questions, and that made him very uneasy, especially since they were so completely interlocked . . .

They'd been driving for ten minutes without speaking when Benjamin, who was at the wheel, said, "We've got company."

"Are you sure?" Markham asked.

"I made two unnecessary turns and they followed."

Markham reached up and adjusted the rearview

mirror to permit him to look at their tail. "Three guys . . . one in the back."

"I only saw the two in the front," Benjamin answered.

"You want to call for backup?"

"Naw, I want them to make a move," Benjamin said and then added, "For damn sure someone doesn't want us to get to the Navy."

"For sure," Markham responded.

"I'm going to cut onto a highway and open up," Benjamin said. "I expect those guys to do the same."

"You're giving them a chance to get us."

Benjamin glanced at Markham. "That's right. But you're going to get them first. There's a double barrel behind you, in a metal box. Take it out, load it and stick it out my window. Show as little of the muzzle as possible."

Markham readied the shotgun.

"Good!" Benjamin exclaimed when the shotgun was in position. "Now we'll head to the highway." He checked the sideview mirror and turned the wheel hard over to the left. To complete the turn, the car climbed up on the sidewalk and tore up someone's front lawn before it bounced off the curb. Even then Benjamin had to fight the wheel to get control of it again.

"Christ, I'm glad I didn't eat anything," Markham commented.

"You must have eaten something before I called you," Benjamin responded.

"Like I said before, you're a dirty old man."

"Check on our company."

Markham looked up into the rearview mirror.

"They're coming around now."

"The entrance to the highway is a couple of miles from here," Benjamin said.

"You know, I'm beginning to think I'm nuts for doing this on my vacation, when I could be spending it with a beautiful woman."

"You are nuts, but either the job means so much to you that you have to be nuts or you should be pushing papers around in some office."

Markham spotted the highway entrance sign.

"We'll enter in style," Benjamin said, switching on the rotating lights and the siren and flooring the accelerator.

In a matter of moments they were on the highway, doing eighty-five.

"You're a fucking menace!" Markham exclaimed.

Benjamin laughed. "Yeah, I guess I am. Now tell me how our tail is doing?"

"They're as crazy as you are."

"I take that to mean that they're coming up behind us?"

"Yeah, that's right."

"This woman you have stashed away back in the motel, is she just a vacation item or something more?" Benjamin asked, glancing quickly at Markham.

"This is one hell of a time to be talking about a woman!"

"Best time in the world," Benjamin said. "You're playing for real high stakes . . . your life. If you don't know now how you feel about certain things, then you'll never know."

Markham looked up into the mirror. "They're

gaining on us," he said.

"That's because I'm easing off the accelerator," Benjamin told him, reaching over to the dash to turn off the rotating yellow and red lights and the siren.

"They just switched lanes; they're coming up on your left."

Moments rushed by and then the car sped up alongside them.

Markham saw the glint of a gun barrel. He shoved the shotgun forward and simultaneously squeezed both triggers. The sound of the blast thundered in the confined space and the gun slammed back into his side, sending a burst of pain through his stomach that doubled him up.

The car continued to move with them for a few seconds, then suddenly it swerved to the left, shot across the grass meridian and slamming into a concrete post, it stopped and burst into flames.

"My God, cars are screeching to a halt or slamming into each other. There must have been a dozen collisions!"

Benjamin slowed down and uttered a deep sigh of relief. "You scared?" he asked.

"Shitless," Markham said.

Benjamin dug a handkerchief out of his back pocket and dabbed the sweat off his forehead. "Me too," he admitted; then he said, "You never got the chance to answer my question about your lady friend."

"I don't intend to answer it," Markham said.

Benjamin laughed. "You already did, son. You already did!"

*   *   *

Benjamin shook hands with Captain Pilcher, a huge black man big enough to be a professional linebacker. Then Markham did the same.

"If you gentlemen will follow me," Pilcher said, "we will be meeting with Vice Admiral Stanley Corliss, ONI's ranking officer here."

The three of them went up one flight of steps, down a well-lit corridor and finally to a wooden door that had Corliss's name on it, and under it the words, "Commanding Officer."

The secretary's desk was unoccupied and Pilcher led them to another door and knocked on it.

"Come in," a man called from the other side of the door.

Pilcher opened the door. "Please, gentlemen," he said, indicating that Benjamin and Markham should precede them into the admiral's office.

Pilcher immediately followed, closed the door behind him and made the introductions. "Admiral Corliss, Detective Lieutenant Charles Benjamin and Detective Guy Markham, of the NYPD."

The admiral's office was a large room, with two windows, a dark wood executive-type desk with the American flag on one side and his own standard, with its three stars, on the other. There was a deep pile blue wall-to-wall carpet on the floor, several naval-type photographs on the walls, a large photograph of the President and the Secretary of the Navy. And on platforms coming out of the wall in various places were models of a variety of warships, including two submarines, one attack and one boomer.

The admiral greeted them with vigorous hand-shakes and bade them to sit down in chairs around a coffee table at the far side of the room rather than those chairs close to the desk. He himself settled in the only leather club chair before he said, "Please smoke if you want to."

Benjamin worked the cellophane off a cigar and said, "My partner in crime here doesn't smoke and eats salads."

Corliss laughed. "Captain Pilcher does the same and runs eight miles a day. Just the thought of doing that exhausts me."

"Just hearing about that has the same effect on me," Benjamin said, lighting up.

"Captain Pilcher has told me an amazing story—" the admiral began.

"It's no story," Benjamin said, cutting him short. "Ten men were on the *Command One* who shouldn't have been there."

"Ten? I thought you supposedly ID'd four?" He looked at Pilcher, who was seated on a small couch across from him.

"There's no doubt that the remaining six will be ID'd the same way," Markham offered.

"May I see the proof you have concerning the four?" Corliss asked.

Benjamin opened his envelope and, taking the folders out, he put them down on the coffee table. "You will see a picture of each dead man and the matching picture with a member of the submarine's crew, and in this folder," he said, "are the FBI's fingerprint reports. The prints of three of the dead men, those are the men who had been killed here in Norfolk, have been matched to members of the submarine's crew and they belong to three of the

112

men in the photographs. The fourth man was killed in Staten Island and we do not have the fingerprint report from the Bureau, but we do have a match between the photographs of the dead man and a member of the submarine's crew." He opened the folders and pushed them gently toward the admiral.

"Astounding!" Corliss said after looking at the photographs. "Captain, please." And he handed them to Pilcher.

"And there's another bit of astounding information," Benjamin said. "A couple of nights ago, a car exploded. The explosion was caused by a bomb and the car was rented to a Captain John Tull—"

"But Tull is the XO on the *Command One*!" Corliss exclaimed.

"I saw his name and picture on the TV news too," Benjamin said, nodding. "Now here's the kicker, how could Tull be on the submarine and in the car at the same time?"

"Tull couldn't have been replaced," Corliss responded.

"I didn't think so. But then that leaves the question of who the man in the car was and who planted the bomb."

"Captain Tull?"

"I don't know," Benjamin said. "But I can tell you that we have a slightly different problem than when I first spoke to Captain Pilcher."

"How's that?" Corliss asked.

"Someone tried to stop us from coming here."

"Stop you?"

"Kill us," Markham said.

"And—" Corliss began, leaving the rest of the

question unstated.

"They're dead," Benjamin answered.

Corliss scanned the photographs again; then he said, "The *C-1* is down, that means whoever tried to kill you was trying to protect either themselves or others."

"In this kind of situation," Markham said, "the hit men are the front line troops."

"Then the two of you are still in danger?" Pilcher said, though the rise in his voice turned the statement into a question.

Markham looked at Benjamin. "I would say so, wouldn't you?"

"Maybe, maybe not. I think it depends on other circumstances."

Everyone waited for him to continue.

"Whoever wanted us dead, wanted to stop us from coming here. They either know by now they failed, or they certainly will know by the time the late news is on TV tonight. Once they know they failed, they no longer have a reason for wanting to kill us unless—"

"They want revenge," Corliss suggested.

"I have a better reason," Benjamin said, taking the cigar out of his mouth and pointing it at the admiral. "The mission isn't completed."

"What mission?" Pilcher questioned.

"The ten impostors were put aboard the submarine to do something. I don't think there's any doubt about that."

"But the *Command One* is down in eighteen thousand feet of water," Corliss said.

"Are you absolutely sure?"

Corliss stood up.

"She sent a May Day," Pilcher said.

Still looking at the admiral, Benjamin repeated the question.

Corliss sat down again. "You're suggesting that *Command One* is not down, but in the hands of— It's unthinkable!"

"Obviously not, Admiral. I just thought of it."

For several moments no one spoke.

"That submarine has state-of-the-art electronic equipment on it," Corliss said in a low voice.

"Does it need a full complement to operate it . . . I mean actually sail it?" Benjamin questioned.

Corliss looked questioningly at Pilcher. "You've been closer to it than I have."

"It's highly automated. The answer is *yes*, it can be operated with less than a full crew. But I can't tell you the minimum number of men that would be needed."

"Get on it now," Corliss ordered.

"Yes, sir," Pilcher responded, leaving his chair and heading to the desk where the phone was located.

"Then you're suggesting that the May Day was a ruse?" Corliss questioned, looking at Benjamin again.

"It's possible."

"What about the crew, the admiral's staff and the general's?"

Benjamin shrugged. "I don't have definitive answers," he said, rolling the cigar from the right side of his mouth to the left. "But—"

"Sir, I just spoke to Captain Wasko at COMSUB-

LANT," Pilcher said, rejoining the group around the coffee table, but not sitting down again. "The bottom line is twelve men and two officers."

Corliss motioned him to sit down.

"The other scenario is that the May Day was real and the submarine is really down in eighteen thousand feet of water," Benjamin said. "There is also a third, but then all of us would have to believe in miracles and, at my age, I find that—well, unfortunately, impossible."

"If what you've just suggested is anywhere near the reality of what has happened and still is happening, then the two of you are still in danger, great danger."

Benjamin shrugged and looked at Markham for an answer.

"The two of us have been there before," the young detective said.

"I'm sure you have," Corliss responded and, getting to his feet, he extended his hand to Benjamin. "As the saying goes, Lieutenant, you gave us the ball."

Benjamin stood up and shook his hand. "I want the killer and I want the guy who gave the orders."

"If we agree that your suggestions have some validity," Corliss said, "the FBI and other agencies will become involved."

"As long as they let me do my job, I don't care who becomes involved."

Corliss laughed. "I was almost sure that you'd give me that kind of a response. I want to thank you and Detective Markham for coming here and congratulate you for your fine work. I will certainly make it a point that each of you receive a letter of commendation."

"You may have the photographs and the Bureau's print reports," Benjamin said. "I have additional sets."

Corliss thanked him.

They'd reached the door before Benjamin said, "Once the ball begins to bounce, tell the guys in those other agencies I don't want to have to push them out of the way, but I will, if they crowd me."

Corliss nodded. "I'll tell them." Then he added, "You're a hard man, Lieutenant."

Benjamin shook his head. "I just like to finish what I start."

10

Smith moved his head from side to side. His vision was blurred, but he was sure someone was bending over him. He was very thirsty and when he tried to ask for water, his throat rasped and the words sounded strange. He had been dreaming, or thinking about his wife Peggy, their marriage, when he sensed that someone was close by and began to move his head from side to side.

"You have to be down for another few hours," Tull said. "A day and a half at the most."

Smith recognized the voice. "Water?" he croaked.

Tull poured water into a glass and held it to his lips.

Smith drank most of it before he realized his hands were tied and Tull was holding the glass for him.

"Need to piss," Smith said, spilling water down the front of his coveralls.

Tull nodded, pulled him up to his feet and, supporting him, led him into the head, just outside the cabin. "I'm going to untie your hands, Captain. But if you make one threatening move, I'll deck you."

"Understand," Smith said.

Tull stepped back and let the man urinate and, as soon as he was finished, retied his hands.

"The other officers?" Smith questioned.

"Same condition as yourself," Tull said, putting him back in his bunk. "The crew is too. Everyone, except myself, Forbushe and ten men."

"Then—"

"It's a planned operation," Tull told him.

Smith shook his head with disbelief and dismay. That a naval officer would betray the country was almost beyond his ability to understand.

"As soon as we reach our destination, all the officers and men will be returned to the United States."

Again Smith shook his head. "You're giving away everything," he croaked, halting between words. "Everything!" Tears streamed out of his eyes.

"Not giving it away. Selling it," Tull said. "It's strictly a business proposition."

Smith felt himself drifting away—in a swirl, where Peggy was waiting. He forced himself back to face Tull. "There's no way out for you, John. No way. I'm sorry." And then Tull dissolved and he was moving toward his wife . . .

11

Tull entered the control room to relieve Forbushe and said, "We'll be changing course in two hours." Despite the fact that he was now working closely with him and had no real reason to complain, he still didn't like Forbushe.

"According to the navigation computer, in exactly one hour and forty-eight minutes," Forbushe answered.

Tull ran his eyes over the various instruments. They were still running at fifteen hundred feet, doing forty knots. "Looks good," he commented.

"When we change course, I'm going to increase our speed to forty-five knots," Forbushe said. "I want to move—"

Tull glanced at the other men on duty. One manned the sonar station, the other was at the diving station. "The faster we go," Tull said, "the louder we are."

"The faster we go, the sooner we'll be finished with this mission. You're getting tired and so am I. If we can cut a few hours off—"

"We damn well might be cutting our nose to spite our face," Tull said. "Even doing forty knots makes one hell of a racket."

"This boat was refitted to be quiet."

"I was even thinking of decreasing the speed when we got close to the toll booth, with the hope that we might slip through before any of the—" He was going to say, our guys, but caught himself and said, "The American boats up there get suspicious."

"Officially we're down," Forbushe responded. "They'll either take us for another American boomer, or a Russian whose sound signature is a very good imitation of an American boomer."

Tull ran his hand across his chin. There wasn't any sense in going eyeball to eyeball with him now. "Let's defer making a decision on it until we're closer to the toll booth."

"I just wanted to let you know what I intend doing."

That was an unmistakable challenge. Tull could hear the sudden booming of his heart. There was just too much at stake to risk blowing it now by arguing with Forbushe. Aware that the two men on duty were intently watching and listening to them, Tull had no choice but to meet Forbushe's challenge. "Wrong time and wrong place, Mister Forbushe," he said in a low hard voice.

"Don't give me that Mister Forbushe shit. Neither one of us are in the fucking Navy anymore."

Tull slammed his fist into Forbushe's stomach. "Stay where you are!" he shouted to the men on duty.

122

Gagging, Forbushe doubled up.

"If we were in 'the fucking Navy' as you put it, I wouldn't have done that. But you're right, we're not. But until this boat is turned over to the people who hired us, I'm its skipper. I make the decisions."

Forbushe glared at him.

"You don't much like me," Tull said, "and I sure as hell don't like you. But I'm the driver."

Without a word, Forbushe abruptly turned around and left the control room.

Tull stared after him and shook his head; then he looked at each man. Neither one would engage his eyes.

"I think this calls for a dinner," Benjamin said as he pulled into the parking area, adjacent to the motel. "You and your lady friend are my guests tonight."

"I'll get Karin—no, why don't you come up to the room with me and I'll introduce the two of you," Markham responded before they got out of the car.

"Be delighted to," Benjamin answered.

The two of them entered the motel lobby and rode the elevator up to the tenth floor.

"Hang a right. I have the corner room, near the stairwell," Markham said.

A woman suddenly shouted, "Oh no . . . no more!"

"Karin!" Markham exclaimed, stopping to pull the .38 from the leg holster.

Benjamin had yanked his weapon free from the belt holster.

The two of them moved toward the door.

Benjamin signaled he'd go first.

Markham shook his head, got in front of him and whispered, "Cover me!" The next instant he was inside the room and three men wearing black ski masks were there.

Naked, Karin was on her stomach in the bed. One man was on top of her, the second held her hands and the third held her legs.

Markham fired at the man on top of Karin. The back of his head splashed over the bed's backboard, while his twitching body rolled off Karin, to the right.

The other two let go of her and went for their weapons.

Benjamin fired two shots.

One man dropped to the floor and the third crashed through the glass sliding door.

The man on the floor struggled to get to his feet.

Benjamin squeezed off another round.

The man slumped to the floor.

Markham pulled Karin to her feet.

"They did it to me," she cried hysterically. "They fucked me; they used my ass. They—"

"Easy, honey," he said gently. "Easy!" He lifted her into his arms, carried her into the bathroom and wrapped a towel around her. The back of her legs was stained with blood.

"An ambulance is on its way," Benjamin called out.

"They said it was payback for what you did," she wept.

Markham turned on the cold water, wet a washcloth and washed her face.

"I thought it was you when they knocked," she told him. "I was only wearing one of your shirts." She began to cry.

He held her close.

"I feel so dirty," she sobbed. "So dirty."

Markham caressed her head. "I love you," he said softly.

She shook her head.

He had seen other women who had experienced the trauma of rape and understood the degradation that Karin was feeling.

"I need to shower," she said.

"I'll get your clothes and then we'll go to the hospital," he told her.

"Must I?" she questioned, tears wetting her cheeks again.

Markham nodded and, stepping out of the bathroom, he closed the door behind him. There were half a dozen cops in the room and two men in white jackets from the hospital were bent over the dead man sprawled across the bed.

"How is she?" Benjamin asked.

"Torn up physically and psychologically. The bastards sodomized her."

"They won't be doing anything to anyone anymore," Benjamin said.

"They told her it was 'payback' for what we did."

"I never figured they'd go for her."

"Neither did I," Markham responded, gathering up her clothes. "I want to take her down to the hospital. Do you have a rape specialist on the force?"

Benjamin nodded. "She's probably off duty. But

I'll get her to come down and speak to Karin."

"Not in the station house."

"Where?"

"In her home?" Markham said.

"You got it," Benjamin answered.

"You sure?"

"I'm sure," Benjamin said. "She's my ex-wife." Then in a much softer voice, he added, "It's alright; she'll do it. She went through it herself. She understands."

Markham uttered a deep sigh and returned to the bathroom. He knocked softly on the door.

Karin didn't answer.

He listened for the sound of the shower, but couldn't hear it. He called again.

No answer.

"Karin?" he called loudly; then he turned the knob and flung open the door. "Oh my God!" he exclaimed. Karin had used his razor to slash her wrists. She was slumped over the sink. "Medic," he shouted, running to her. He grabbed hold of her wrists; the cuts on both of them were jagged.

One of the paramedics from the ambulance pushed past him. "I'll get a tourniquet on those cuts," he said. "Put her clothes on and we'll get her to the hospital.

"I want to die," Karin wept. "Please let me die!"

The paramedic stopped the flow of blood and put bandages on both her wrists; then Markham dressed her. "I'm going to the hospital with her," he told Benjamin. "You contact your ex-wife and get her to the hospital."

"She'll be there," Benjamin responded.

"I want those guys. The ones who gave the orde.
to do this to her," Markham said in a flat, hard
voice. "I want them, Charles, and I'll stay here until I
get them."

"I'm sure something can be arranged with your
command," Benjamin said.

Markham nodded, lifted Karin into his arms and
carried her out of the bathroom.

"I'm dirty," she wept, holding tight to him
and pressing her face into his chest. "I'm dirty.
Dirty . . ."

Markham sucked in his breath and slowly
exhaled. Now he had something to pay back. On the
way out of the lobby, he saw Pilcher.

"I came as soon as Lieutenant Benjamin called the
admiral," he said, looking at Karin.

"She'll be alright," Markham said. "The lieutenant is upstairs in the room."

Pilcher nodded. "Good luck," he said, already
moving away.

Markham climbed into the back of an ambulance
and, still cradling Karin, he sat down. "Go," he
called out. "Go!"

"I'm sorry to have taken you away from your
guests," Brett Hubbered said, referring to the state
dinner being given in honor of Mexico's president.
"But we have something that has come up with
regard to the *Command One* that demands your
attention."

The President nodded and walked with a deter-
mined stride. He had taken office in January and

still was, by his own admission, wet behind the ears.

"Admiral Corliss—"

"Corliss?" the President questioned, glancing at Hubbered, who had been one of the architects of his victory.

"Head of the Office of Naval Intelligence," Hubbered said. "And Vice Admiral Hicks, commander of COMSUBLANT, our fleet of submarines in the Atlantic."

They reached the Oval Office and Hubbered opened the door for the President.

The two admirals immediately stood up.

"Gentlemen, please make yourselves comfortable," the President said, going behind his desk. "Excuse the formal getup," he said. "But state dinners aren't given in a casual manner, though before my term of office is up, I just might do it." He laughed. "Could you imagine the field day that the gossip columnists of this town would have with that?"

Hubbered said, "Mister President, Admiral Corliss has some startling information to reveal to you . . . Admiral?"

Corliss opened his black leather attaché case and removed the set of photographs and prints that Benjamin had given to him. "These photographs," he explained, "are of three John Does—three men who were brutally murdered in the Norfolk area. And these, Mister President, are photographs of three men who are missing aboard the *Command One*."

A moment passed before the President exclaimed,

"By Christ, they're the same. But how could that be?"

Corliss laid out the situation exactly the way Benjamin had presented it to him hours before, including the attempt to kill the two detectives and the subsequent rape of a young woman, with whom the detective from New York was involved.

The President listened carefully; then, when Corliss was finished, he placed the palms of his hands together and, fixing his elbows on the arms of his swivel-back chair, he said, "So we have ten imposters and a captain who might be involved in a bombing aboard a downed submarine."

Corliss nodded.

"There are some questions raised by this, Mister President," Hicks said.

"Yes, Admiral, what are they?" the President said. He himself had graduated from Annapolis and had seen action over Hanoi, where he'd earned the Air Medal by shooting down three MIGs in one dog fight and later a Navy Cross for having stayed with his wing man and prevented his capture by the enemy until he'd been rescued by a chopper.

"We don't know who is responsible for the killings. We don't know if they have placed impostors anywhere else. We don't know anything about them."

The President nodded. "Right now, I think the question is whether or not we believe *Command One* is really down, or was that signal a ruse?"

"According to the information I have obtained," Corliss said, "that submarine can be operated with a minimum of ten men—that doesn't mean she can function on the level that she could with a full complement, but she can be sailed."

"She certainly can," Hicks said, answering a questioning look from the President.

The President ran his fingers through his black wavy hair. "Ten men murdered, another murdered aboard the submarine and then a chopper blown out of the sky with the loss of four men. Fifteen men and one innocent woman brutally assaulted—I'd give ten to one that May Day was a ruse."

Both admirals stirred uneasily in the chairs and Hicks said, "With all due respect to this new era of friendship with the Russians, but getting possession of *Command One* would save them years of research, to say nothing of giving them detailed information about our command operational capabilities."

Hubbered agreed with him.

Corliss played much closer to the vest. "There are other countries that could have engineered this—countries in the Middle East, for example."

The President leaned forward. "'The question is whether or not we can find *Command One* and regain control of her?"

"She's very fast," Hicks said. "Only the fastest attack submarines can match her speed."

"Is she armed?"

"No,"

"Well, that's something in our favor," the President commented.

"If the Russians are behind this," Hicks said, "she only has two ways of getting to a Russian port safely.

130

One is through the northern passageway and the other is through the Mediterranean to the Black Sea."

"We can seal the Med with the Sixth Fleet easily enough—that's if they're not through the Strait of Gibraltar."

"They could head for Vladivostok," Hubbered suggested, "either around the Horn or the Cape of Good Hope."

"Either of those two routes would put a tremendous strain on a dozen men," Corliss said. "They'd either try for a Black Sea port, or one in the north—Murmansk, or maybe even Kronstadt. Either of those would make more sense from a time consideration."

The President stood up and, as was his wont when he was thinking hard about something, he began to pace behind the desk. "It would be to our advantage to force them to use either of the long routes to get to a Russian port, that is, if the Russians are behind it, which I doubt." Suddenly he stopped. "What does the method of mutilation suggest to you?"

"A sexual reason for the crime, or rather to make it look as if there was one," Hubbered said.

"It has in the past been used by certain groups of people to indicate their hatred for individuals not of their religious and political persuasion."

"An Arab country?"

"A possibility," the President answered, resuming his pacing.

The room was silent, except for the ticking of a large grandfather clock and padding of the President's feet as he paced.

131

"But that too—the mutilation could have been done to make us think that agents of a Middle Eastern nation were responsible," the President said, without stopping his pacing. "No, I don't think we can settle on one or another possibility. We must take whatever action we must to find and regain control of the *Command One* and, failing that, destroy it. We have already announced that it is down; therefore, if we have to destroy it we need not reveal it. But we must proceed on the basis that there are two different players in this situation, namely Russia and a second, belonging to the Arab world." He stopped and rested his hands on the back of the chair. "The longer we force the pirates—and that's exactly what they are—to remain at sea, then the stronger the possibility that fatigue will dull their edge and permit the members of the submarine's crew to overcome them and retake it."

"Mr. President, I will notify the Secretary of the Navy and the Chief of Naval Operations that you have ordered the Sixth Fleet to—"

"Carry on standard maneuvers on the Atlantic side of the Strait of Gibraltar. I want both our aircraft carriers involved—make that every warship in the fleet. I will personally discuss the matter with Sir Hugh Corbet, the British ambassador."

"Yes, Mister President," Hubbered answered.

"To cover ourselves in the North Atlantic," the President said, "we'll begin unannounced maneuvers in that area. Get as many ships and submarines as you can between Greenland and Norway."

"Admiral Hicks, how many attack submarines can you put out there?" the President asked.

"Forty."

"Send them north immediately," the President said.

"Yes, Mister President," Hicks answered.

"Brett, have every attack submarine we have in the Pacific head toward the Vladivostok. We'll meet again tomorrow at nine o'clock in the morning. Brett, see that the CNO, and the heads of the CIA and FBI are also present. Now, I must return to my guests. Good night, gentlemen." He nodded to them. "Please, don't stand," he said as he stepped out from behind the desk and headed for the door.

A black Mercedes sedan slowed and stopped at the corner of Seaside Drive and 80th Street. The back door opened and a man hurried out of the shadows of an alleyway and settled in the backseat. Even before the door was pulled shut, the car's wheels squealed into motion.

"What is the situation?" the man next to the driver asked. English was obviously his second language.

"The hunt is on," the man who entered the car said. "You made a mistake—two mistakes: you should have never tried to stop those two detectives and you should have never sent those men to rape that woman."

"Had we stopped the detectives we would have bought more time," the driver answered. He too spoke with an accent.

"Now they're looking for you," the man in the backseat answered.

"How could they be looking for us, when they

don't know who they're looking for?" the man next to the driver asked.

"Leave this area. Go to New York."

"What about the hunt?" the driver asked.

"They're putting everything into position. They've guessed the Russian's are responsible, but they have not ruled out the possibility that it may be the work of an Arab nation."

The man in the front chuckled. "Always politics, eh. It would never cross their minds that it could be the work of independents. Right now, our negotiators have received a very good bid from Libya . . . but Syria has asked for time to rethink its position."

"And the Soviets?" the man in the rear questioned.

"They've stood firm with their initial offer of five hundred million. But I think the Libyans will top that. In twelve hours' time, we'll send a signal to Tull and tell him where to make the final delivery."

The man in the backseat didn't say anything.

"We might have to put a full crew aboard at sea," the man next to the driver said. "But the people with whom we're in contact said that would be no problem. Once a foreign crew is aboard and she's under a foreign flag, then the United States would be placed in a very difficult position. If she fires on the submarine, she is committing an act of war and of course risks killing her own people."

"What will happen to the crew?"

"If either Libya or Syria get the submarine, they get the crew too and all of them become hostages."

The man in the rear closed his eyes and leaned back into the seat. Just to think of having millions of dollars at his disposal was almost like thinking about making love to a beautiful woman. "The next seventy-two to ninety-six hours are critical," he commented, more to himself than to the other men in the car. Then he said, "My car is at the Waterside Holiday Inn. You can drop me off there."

Neither of the two men in front answered.

He opened his eyes and found himself looking at the muzzle of a gun capped with a silencer. The loud pop and the pain came together. Then more pain . . .

The man next to the driver put away the gun, reached into the backseat and put the body against the door. "Slow down and stay in the center lane." He waited until he saw a car moving in behind them in the right lane. "Now," he said and, opening the door, he pushed the body into the path of the oncoming car.

Benjamin and Markham waited in the eighth-floor waiting room of the hospital. It was already 11:30 and Elizabeth—Liz—had been with Karin since ten.

The waiting room emptied out after visiting hours ended, leaving only the two of them. Markham made several dozen trips between the windows in one wall and the glass in the other that gave him a view of the closed door of Karin's room.

"You're going to be a very tired man," Benjamin said, smoking his fourth cigar of the evening.

"The damndest thing is that I really love her," Markham commented, looking out of the window.

"You sure?"

"I was going to ask her to come back to New York

135

with me," Markham said. "We'd live together for a while and if it worked—well, you know how it goes." He faced Benjamin.

"I know how it goes," Benjamin answered.

"What about you and Elizabeth?"

Benjamin shrugged.

"She seems like a wonderful person and she's really good-looking."

"She's only forty . . . five years younger than I am."

"You look a hell of a lot older."

Benjamin released smoke through his nostrils. "You're full of compliments," he said.

"What I meant—"

Benjamin waved his hand. "You're right. I look old enough to be her father." He took the cigar out of his mouth. "Two years ago she was raped."

Markham moved to one of the chairs facing Benjamin.

"Someone we both knew," Benjamin said. "We were out at a party. I got a call and had to leave. She stayed and this guy named Philip offered to drive her home after the party. By the time they left, he had more than just one or two drinks. As soon as they were on the road, he put his hand on her thigh and said he always had a yen for her. She laughed and told him that she was flattered. He started to push her dress up high and said he was taking her to a motel. She pushed his hand away and told him that she wasn't going to any motel with him. He turned off the highway and on to a country road, where he stopped the car and slapped her across the face several times. Then he raped her." Benjamin put the

136

cigar back in his mouth and puffed hard on it. "When it got down to the bottom line, it was her word against his."

"What about sperm tests?" Markham questioned.

"Liz showered as soon as she got home. The next morning, when I finally came home, I found her sitting on the couch in her bathrobe. Gradually I was able to get her to tell me what had happened."

"So?"

"Philip told me she didn't fight him. She wanted him to fuck her."

"Did she fight—"

Benjamin shook his head. "Philip is two hundred and eight pounds. He was on top of her and had one of his mitts over her mouth. She had all she could do to breathe. She was afraid he'd kill her if she fought him."

"He very well could have," Markham said.

"I couldn't hack it. Everyone who was at the party knew that Philip had screwed her. That was his story and most of the people believed him. I couldn't go near her without seeing Philip on top of her, or Philip's hand where mine had been."

Markham shook his head. "What about her? How did she react?"

"It no longer worked for either of us," Benjamin said as he took the cigar out of his mouth and looked toward the door, which was opening.

Liz waved to him and he left the waiting room. "She wants to see you," Liz told him; then with a gentle smile, she said, "She'll be fine after a while."

He started to go into the room, but Liz took hold of his arm. "She's been through a lot and has a lot

137

more to go through, but if you're willing to wait, she'll be there to love you."

"Thanks, really, thanks for coming here," he told her.

She bobbed her head toward the waiting room. "How is he?"

"Tired and sad, I think. Maybe a whole lot guilty."

She looked toward the waiting room.

"He told me," Markham said softly. "He needs you."

Her eyebrows went up. "He told you that?" she asked in a small, choked voice.

"Not in so many words," Markham said. "But he does. It's not too late . . ."

12

More than an hour later, Forbushe's stomach still ached from Tull's savage blow. He sat at his desk in the engineering office, waiting for the men he'd summoned to join him. That he'd allowed Tull to strike him in front of two of the men without fighting back was certainly a loss of face which might in the future prove difficult to overcome. But to him the mission came first. He was a patient man, especially when patience was required to deal with an enemy. And Tull, despite the fact that they were on the same mission, had become his enemy.

With some difficulty, Forbushe leaned back in the chair. He knew all about Commander John Tull. As soon as he had been notified by his superior, Admiral Akara Mohammed Karim, as to who would be in command, he'd had, through his various contacts, procured a complete dossier on the captain.

It had been his opinion from the beginning and still was that Tull had been a poor choice. The man was one of the few remaining, as he referred to them, swashbucklers left—agents who had gotten their training in the late sixties and early seventies in southeast Asia, rather than in the more sophisticated training of the Middle East arena.

According to Tull's dossier, he'd been turned sometime in 1980, while serving as assistant naval attaché in Moscow. He'd become involved with Galena Trotsky, a distant relation to Leon Trotsky, the man who had been one of the leaders in the Russian Revolution and who was later assassinated in Mexico by Stalin's gunmen. Galena had been KGB and had gotten him to go over. In 1985, while Tull had been on a vacation trip to Paris he met a Francene Ughett, who introduced him to a Syrian agent and agreed to pass certain sensitive information to him. Tull, of course, had to have the approval of his KGB control to do this. But since the Soviet and Syrian interests in the Middle East coincided, he had no trouble becoming a double agent. But Tull's problem, as the compiler of the dossier so astutely pointed out, was women. He apparently could be characterized as a satyr, and women found him magnetically irresistible. The dossier also stated that he had no interest in political or religious ideology. The motive for his actions was strictly financial and, the report stated, "This did not lessen his performance, in fact it may have increased it . . ." Recalling those words made Forbushe grimace. As far as he was concerned, a man without a political ideology was a man without a central core, with a hollowness that could easily be filled, and that was dangerous.

A soft knock interrupted his thoughts. "Come," he answered.

The two men who had been on duty in the control room when Tull had struck him entered and were immediately followed by two more.

"Smoke, if you wish," Forbushe said. With some difficulty, he moved forward. "What's the situation?" he asked, looking at the men who had been in the control room.

"We are approaching the turning point," one of them answered. He looked at his watch. "We should make it in ten minutes."

Forbushe nodded. "At this speed we'll probably feel it and we'll have to trim the mark again to maintain our depth."

None of the men commented. Two of them had occupied the two chairs and two leaned against the bulkhead. One of them lit a cigarette and another a pipe.

"Tull must be dealt with," Forbushe said.

"I will kill him now," the man, who had been at the sonar when Tull struck Forbushe, said.

"No, he is still needed," Forbushe said. "He has the skill to bring us through—"

"He plans to head north," the other man said. "Our way is through the Strait of Gibraltar."

"In another few hours we will head toward the surface, periscope depth, and send a coded signal. The answer will tell us which way to go. Once we know our new course, we will act and then Tull will have to get us past the Sixth Fleet and to our rendezvous point."

"I say kill him now and get it over with," the sonar

141

operator said. "He is—"

"Not until I say so," Forbushe snapped.

"I would not let any man strike me and then do nothing about it," the man responded sullenly.

"You will not kill him," Forbushe said, his voice going flat and hard and his eyes narrowing to slits. "I will kill him myself and I will do it so that he knows it is me."

The sonar operator nodded.

Suddenly the 1MC came on. "All hands now hear this . . . All hands now hear this . . . We are making a one-hundred-and-eight-degree turn to the port side."

"He still thinks he's in the Navy," one of the men laughed.

All of them joined him and Forbushe said, "Our strength is to let him think whatever he wants to, as long as he does what must be done to successfully bring this submarine to where we want it to be brought."

13

It was 3 A.M. when Benjamin and Markham were looking at Pilcher's broken body in the gutter.

Razzili the coroner was there. "He was shot to death first, then dumped."

Benjamin made no comment, but Markham said, "I noticed he was in civvies when I met him in the lobby of the motel."

"These last few days I've been busier than I've been in the last year," Razzili told them.

"What about the gunshot wounds?" Benjamin asked.

"Close range. Maybe two feet away at the most. Nothing big, probably a .38. And my guess is that the weapon had a silencer on it. If it didn't, the guy, or guys, who did it have a bad case of ringing in their ears, or a temporary deafness."

Benjamin fished a cheap cigar out of his breast pocket and lit it. He had left the hospital with Liz and had taken her back to his apartment. When the call had come about Pilcher from Headquarters, they had just fallen asleep in each other's arms. He had left her in bed and he hoped she'd be there when he returned.

"Poor bastard never had a chance," Markham commented.

"Before I forget," Razzilli said, "that guy who was in the car that blew up—"

"Yeah, what about him?"

"A Ruskie."

"What the fuck are you talking about?" Benjamin questioned, rolling the cigar from the right side of his mouth to his left. Because making love to Liz had been good, he was more than annoyed that he had been roused from bed; he was almost angry about it. This time none of the ugly images had come into his brain; this time she had been more important than his job.

Razzilli nodded. "A Ruskie."

"For Christ sake, there wasn't enough of him left to tell whether he was man or a fucking hermaphrodite and you're telling me he was a Ruskie."

"The lower part of the jaw had capped teeth."

"So."

"The last four digits of his ID number were engraved on the caps," Razzili said. "I turned them over to the FBI. Seems they had a very large file on him. His real name was Serge Petrove."

Markham let out a low whistle.

"You're absolutely sure about this?" Benjamin asked.

"Absolutely. You can check on it by calling Agent Terry Jarvis at the Bureau in Washington."

Suddenly Benjamin smiled and, slapping Razzilli on the back, he exclaimed, "Good work, Doc. Damn good work!" Then, pointing his cigar at Markham, he said, "I think the first thing we better do tomorrow—I mean this morning—is do some checking on Commander John Tull."

"Who the hell is Commander John Tull?" Razzilli asked.

"That's what we're going to try to find out," Benjamin said. "Not only who, but also what—the what may prove to be more interesting than the who."

"I'd be willing to bet," Razzilli said, "this killing is connected to those three John Does."

"How much?" Benjamin asked.

"How much what?"

"Money. How much would you be willing to bet?" Markham questioned.

Suddenly Razzilli began to laugh. "They are, aren't they?"

"You should have been a detective," Benjamin said.

And the three of them laughed.

Benjamin looked beyond the police barriers. The TV crews were already moving around with cameras, lights and a microphone, and the newspaper reporters were also waiting with their tape recorders. "What the hell do I tell them this time?"

"Tell them you have some interesting information," Markham suggested.

"That's certainly true," Razzilli commented.

Benjamin nodded. "By God, it is true." And

145

walking up to face the TV reporters, he hoped his wife was watching.

Later, as Benjamin drove Markham back to the motel, he said, "You didn't sound as if you had been sleeping when I called you."

"I wasn't. I was out on the terrace doing some thinking."

Benjamin was quiet for a few moments before he said, "You're going to marry Karin, aren't you?"

"Yeah, if she wants to?"

"Suppose she doesn't," Benjamin offered. "Suppose she feels that she can't, at least for a while."

"I expect her to say that."

Benjamin glanced at him. "I guess if you care that much about her, there's no other way to go."

"There's no other way for me to go," Markham answered.

Benjamin stopped for a red light.

"What about you and Liz?" Markham questioned.

"It might work," he answered, grinning wolfishly. "It might work. I need her, I realize that now."

"Did you tell her?"

"I told her," Benjamin said, moving on the green light.

"And what was her answer?" Markham asked.

"Hell, you want to know too damn much," Benjamin said; then he added, "I left her in bed."

Markham nodded with obvious satisfaction.

"To change the subject," Benjamin said, "what's

146

your best guess at this time about Commander Tull?"

Markham stretched. "For an American naval officer, he's certainly tied—at least by way of the car—to the wrong person."

"So it would seem," Benjamin responded. "Any thoughts about Captain Pilcher?"

"Probably the same as yours."

"He was connected to the people responsible for the various killing and to the guys who raped Karin."

"And the guys who tried to take us out," Benjamin said. "He probably tipped them off as soon as I finished speaking to him on the phone." He stopped for another light. "Well, at least we know the real Commander Tull is on the submarine."

"That may not be all that good."

The light changed to green and Benjamin pressed down on the accelerator before he said, "I have a gut feeling that *Command One* isn't down in eighteen thousand feet of water."

Markham responded, "If it isn't, then something very big has gone down."

"Big enough to steal a super submarine?"

"Maybe, if that submarine can be run with only ten men, maybe . . . ?"

"What about the regular crew?"

"Could be dead?"

"Dead? That's a lot of men for only ten men to kill . . . eleven, if Tull is in on it."

"Captured, then."

"Captured, how? By whom? They're on a submarine."

Markham shrugged, but didn't answer.

"On a submarine . . . How can—" He snapped his fingers. "I got it. It can be done."

"Alright, tell me."

"Make them sick. Poison them in some way. Put something in the water, the food. You put time in on a submarine, tell me, could it be done?"

"Yeah, it could be done. But it wouldn't be easy."

Benjamin had to jam on the brake to stop from going through a red light. "That's the only way ten or eleven guys could get control of the submarine. It fits together now. I bet that sub could be operated with ten or eleven men. Guy, that fucking submarine never went down, I'm sure of it now."

"I sure as hell hope you're wrong."

"My gut tells me I'm right and—this is just a wild guess—Tull is the linchpin. Not the boss man, but the linchpin."

"We'll see how close your wild guess is to the truth tomorrow when we do some digging on Tull. But right now, I'm tired and my brain has turned to mush. I can't think straight."

"Okay, okay, I get the message."

Markham closed his eyes and after a while he said, "I know this is crazy to think about at a time like this, but if I tell you what's in my head, do you promise not to laugh."

Slowing for the next red light, Benjamin agreed not to laugh.

"Karin's breasts," Markham said. "They're beautiful and they just fit into my hands."

Benjamin brought the car to a stop and, glancing at Markham, he smiled. He'd just been thinking about how beautiful Liz's breasts were, but he wasn't going to tell Markham that.

"Know what I mean?" Markham asked without opening his eyes.

"Sure," Benjamin answered, taking his foot off the brake and moving to the gas pedal.

The second meeting with the President took place in the war room, where the disposition of every one of America's warships, submarines, missile, bomber and fighter wings, and its various Marine and Army divisions were displayed on a huge electronic wall map of the world. Many of the warships, submarines, missile and aircraft wings and ground units were combat ready.

In addition to the President, Admirals Corliss and Hicks and Mister Hubbered, Mister Harold Otis, the head of the FBI, and Mister Paul Sykes, the Director of the CIA, and the Chief of Naval Operations, Admiral Steven Fletcher, were also seated at the long, highly polished oak table. In front of each man was a small decanter of water, a leather portfolio that held a legal-size lined yellow pad and a ballpoint pen.

"Gentlemen," the President said, "we have the possibility of an armed conflict between ourselves and Russia, or between ourselves and some other nation as a result of the disappearance of our submarine *Command One*. I will ask Admiral Corliss to give us the facts he has uncovered. Admiral, please."

Corliss said, "Before I begin, Mister President, I

was informed early this morning by phone that Captain Jedadeah Pilcher, my aide, had been shot to death last night."

"I'm sorry," the President said. "But I have to ask if the killing was related to the other killings?"

"Yes, Mister President, it appears that it was, and I'm extremely sorry to have to report that it also seems that Captain Pilcher had something to do with the deaths of the other men, the attempted murder of two detectives and the rape of a young woman."

"My God!" the President exclaimed, leaping up and beginning to pace. "How could something like that happen, gentlemen? I mean, how could a man rise to the rank of captain and none of our security people know he's a—damn it, gentlemen, he had to have been an enemy agent."

"Or a free-lancer," Sykes said, speaking in a nasal tone and taking the curved pipe out of his mouth. "There are more of them around than actual enemy agents."

"Whatever the hell he was, we should have known about it," the President countered. He returned to his chair and nodded to Corliss. "I apologize, Admiral, for the interruption."

"I'm afraid, Mister President, the two detectives working on the case—"

"What case?" Otis asked. He was a self-contained-looking man, of middling height, dressed in a dark blue suit, white shirt and a dark blue tie.

"They were investigating the death of three men in the Norfolk area, and when the *Command One* was reported down and photographs of members of her crew were shown on TV, they realized that three matched the dead John Does. Eventually, they managed to ID John Does who were killed in different cities."

"Are you telling me that there are ten men aboard the *Command One* who don't belong there?"

"That's exactly what he's telling," the President said, "and it took two detectives to put it together and bring it to him."

"I spoke to Detective Benjamin at five o'clock this morning, after I was notified about Captain Pilcher," Corliss said. "He filled me in with the details about the rape of the woman. I had already known about the attempt on his life and the life of Detective Markham, who, by the way, is with the New York Police Department and was vacationing in Virginia Beach when he became involved in the initial investigation of the John Does. It now seems, according to Detective Benjamin, that Commander John Tull has come under suspicion."

"Tull? He's the submarine's executive officer," Hicks said.

Corliss nodded.

"Let's have it," the President said.

"The night *Command One* sailed, a car exploded and burned on a stretch of highway between Norfolk and Virginia Beach. From what was left of the driver, he has been ID'd as Serge Petrov, alias Harry Lamb."

"How does that put Commander Tull under suspicion?" Otis questioned.

"The last four digits of his ID number were engraved on the caps of his teeth. He was ID'd by your people, Mister Otis, as KGB."

Otis answered, "I'll certainly check that out."

"The car that Petrov drove was rented to Commander Tull," Corliss said.

The President was on his feet again. "The next thing I expect to hear is that Tull stole *Command One!*"

"That may not be too far off the mark," Corliss responded, "at least according to Detectives Benjamin and Markham, who was a submariner for several years before turning to police work. I checked on him; his record in and out of the service is perfect. He was a CPO when he left and turned down an offer to become an officer."

"I want those two brought here today," the President said. "They seem to know more about what is going on than—" He stopped and looked first at Otis and then at Sykes—"than the people who get paid to know. Tell me what else Detective Benjamin told you."

"He suggested that *Command One* is in the hands of Tull and the ten impostors," Corliss said.

"That's utterly impossible!" Hicks exclaimed.

"Ten men against the entire crew and the staffs of an admiral and a general?" Sykes questioned. "Not possible . . . absolutely not possible."

"The odds are against it," Otis stated.

"Not if the crew was completely neutralized, either through food poisoning or something in the drinking water."

"A damn possibility!" the President exclaimed.

"Nerve gas could have been used too," Corliss said, "though Detective Benjamin did not mention it as a possibility."

The President rubbed his hands together. "Alright, we already have ships moving into an intercept position." His eyes went to the CNO.

"Yes, Mister President, we have elements of the Atlantic Fleet heading north, as you can see from the chart. There are also elements of the Sixth Fleet on the move to block the Atlantic side of the Strait of Gibraltar and we have ships moving toward Vladivostok."

"Elements?"

"Mister President—"

"I don't want elements, Admiral, I want everything we have. I want to stop that submarine from falling into the hands of a foreign power and that foreign power who has engineered this theft will do everything possible to get that submarine into its territorial waters."

"But that would mean stripping—"

"Do it, Admiral, and do it now. Pick up the phone and get our ships into position. We might have a war on our hands in the next twenty-four or forty-eight hours. I want our potential adversaries to realize that we will go toe to toe with them, if it should come to that. Go to full alert. Is that clear?"

"Yes, Mister President," Fletcher answered.

The President nodded and, looking at Sykes and Otis, he said, "For the remainder of this investigation both your departments will be at the disposal of Detectives Benjamin and Markham." His gray eyes shifted to Corliss. "Yours too, Admiral."

"Yes, Mister President."

"As of now, those two men are part of my staff—is

153

that clear to everyone in this room?" the President asked.

Each of the men at the table nodded.

"Mister Hubbered, you take care of the necessary paperwork to make them part of my staff," the President said. "If there are any problems, I don't want to hear about them . . . I want them overcome."

"Yes, Mister President," Hubbered answered.

"Well, gentlemen, I am putting all our armed forces on full alert," the President said. "We are as close to a war as we were during the Cuban Missile Crisis in '62 . . . Mister Hubbered, when the two detectives arrive at the White House, I want them brought to me immediately.

"Yes, Mister President," Hubbered answered.

"If we're very lucky," the President said, "we might avoid a war. But only if we're very lucky." He looked at the clock above the center of the electronic map. "It's 10 A.M. now. We'll meet again at six this evening." Then he turned and started toward the door, but before he reached it, he stopped and, facing the men at the table, he said, "Admiral Fletcher, order the submarine destroyed."

"Mister President, there might be a way—"

"The only way is to destroy it before fighting over it destroys the world. Find it and destroy it," the President ordered.

"Yes, Mister President," Fletcher answered in a low, sad voice.

Benjamin put down the phone. "That was the

head of the National Security Agency," he said, looking at Markham, who was seated on the opposite side of the desk. "We've been ordered to Washington today."

"When today?" Markham asked.

"A Navy chopper will fly us directly to the White House."

"When?"

"Four this afternoon," Benjamin answered. "He also said that the FBI, CIA and ONI are at our complete disposal."

Markham nodded approvingly. "First, before I do anything, I'm going to visit Karin; then I'm going to track Tull's movements."

"Alright. I'll see what I can find out about the single officers," Benjamin said. "They'd be more likely to become involved in something than the married ones."

Markham agreed, stood up and stretched.

"Better be back here by three," Benjamin said.

"Three it is," Markham answered.

"Oh, by the way, I forgot to mention that we're on the President's staff," Benjamin told him.

Markham whirled around and, resting his palms on the edge of the desk, he bent over it, thrusting his face close to Benjamin's. "You just forgot to mention that, right?"

"That doesn't change things. You're still a detective."

"It changes who I'm working for."

"So?"

Markham pulled himself away from the desk and, pointing a finger at Benjamin, he said, "You're fucking impossible, that's what you are."

Benjamin laughed. "That's what gives me a certain style," he answered.

"If you had any style—" Markham shook his head, waved him away and said, "It's just not worth the effort." And he walked out of Benjamin's cubicle.

Laughing, Benjamin called after him. "You wouldn't want to keep your new boss waiting, would you?"

Markham entered the hospital room.

Karin was propped up by two pillows. Her eyes were closed, but there was a slight smile on her face.

He moved to the bed and, bending close to her, he gently kissed her on the lips.

She opened her eyes. "I knew it was you," she said. "I recognized the scent of your cologne."

Standing erect, he took hold of her hand and kissed the back of it.

"The doctor said I could leave the hospital today," she said.

"I have to go to Washington for a few hours," he said, "but I'll be back in time for a late dinner, or maybe a sandwich."

"I can't go back to the motel," she told him.

"You just leave word where you are and I'll—"

"Guy, I want to go home," she said. "I don't want to stay here anymore."

"I understand," he said.

"Will you come with me?" Karin asked.

"I can't, not now . . . not until—" he stopped. The

less she knew the better off she was.

"I thought—" She eased her hand out of his and turned her face away.

Reaching over and putting his hand under her chin, he gently brought her face around to his. "You thought what?" he asked.

"It doesn't matter now," she answered, her eyes beginning to glisten with unshed tears.

"Marry me, Karin," he whispered.

Her eyes widened.

He nodded. "Will you marry me?"

Slowly a smile spread across her lips. "If you'll have me," she answered.

Markham gathered her into his arms. "I love you," he said in a low voice close to her ear.

"It might take a while before—" she began.

He kissed her forehead, her eyelids and then the tip of her nose. "You didn't answer me," he said.

"Yes . . . yes, I'll marry you!"

He took hold of her shoulders. "This has to be proof that I'm not just marrying you for sex alone."

She raised her eyebrows; then, indicating a small space between the thumb and fourth finger of her right hand, she said, "Maybe this much sex?"

He shook his head.

She made a moue. "I wouldn't want to think that I wasn't sexually desirable?"

He laughed. "If you were any more sexually desirable to me, I'd be walking around with a permanent hard-on. But I'm marrying you because I've fallen in love with you."

She reached up and put her arms around his neck. "Me too," she said.

"Good, now that I love you and you love me, you can go home and tell your mom and dad that you're going to marry me."

This time she kissed him. "I'll go back to the motel and wait for you," she said.

"Are you sure?"

She nodded. "I'm sure," she answered.

Markham moved away from her. "I'll see you later tonight," he said, blowing her a kiss from the open door.

14

The first man on Benjamin's list of single officers was Lieutenant Commander William Forbushe, who lived in an apartment at 2420 Hewitt Avenue in Virginia Beach.

"The only thing I can say about him," the landlady said as she unlocked the door to the apartment, "was that he was a quiet one and never smiled, even when he said hello."

"Did he ever have any visitors?" Benjamin asked.

She shook her head. "I don't think he ever brought a lady friend here the way the other single men do. But there was one time, a few months back, when someone drove him home. It was in the early spring. I was looking out of the window when the car pulled up. The man behind the wheel was fat, very fat."

Benjamin thanked her for the information.

"Does he have any next of kin?" she asked.

"I don't know," Benjamin answered. He hadn't considered that possibility.

She looked into the apartment. "If he doesn't—"

He immediately understood what she wanted. "The Navy will take possession of his belongings."

She nodded and backed away. "Yes, that's exactly what I told my husband," she said.

Benjamin excused himself, entered the apartment and closed the door behind him. The apartment consisted of two rooms and a bathroom. He started with the bedroom. There was a bed, two chairs, a dresser and color TV. There weren't any pictures on the walls and the window lacked a curtain, though it did have a shade.

He opened the closet. A mixture of civilian clothes and uniforms, about what he would have expected to find. He went through the pockets of every pair of pants and every jacket and came up with nothing. Then he examined the drawers in the dresser. Out of the three of them, Forbushe only used two and there wasn't much in them. He tore apart the bed and came up dry, not that he had any idea what he was looking for.

The other room served as a combination parlor and kitchen. The actual kitchen space was nothing more than a nook off to one side. He checked the fridge. The only thing in it was a single can of beer. There were some magazines on the kitchen table: *Playboy,* opened to a crotch shot, *Popular Science, People* and *Psychology Today.* All of them were old issues. In the other part of the room there was a couch and two club chairs. All three pieces were old and almost dirty looking. The man had lived a Spartan existence, that was certain; then suddenly Benjamin spotted a matchbook cover on the floor, alongside one of the club chairs. He walked over to the chair and picked up the matchbook cover. It came from the Holiday Inn at Waterside and on the inside Forbushe had neatly printed Tull's name and a phone number.

Benjamin smiled, looked for the phone, didn't find it and remembered that he hadn't seen one in the bedroom either. Pocketing the matchbook cover, he went over the apartment again and discovered that there was a phone jack and guessed that Forbushe had either been ripping the phone company off or had taken the phone with him aboard the submarine, though that didn't seem as logical as his first guess.

When he left Forbushe's apartment, Benjamin drove straight to the Holiday Inn. Before going into the cocktail lounge, he stopped at a telephone and put a call through to Razzili.

"Listen," Benjamin said, "I know you guys can get a fair idea of what a guy looked like from just a few bones."

"You want to know what Petrov looked like?"

"How fat was he?"

"Better than two-fifty, maybe even three hundred," Razzili answered.

"You're sure?"

"A mister five-by-five," Razzili said.

"Thanks," Benjamin said. "Thanks a lot." Then he hung up and dialed the number inside the matchbook cover. The line was busy. He hung up, pocketed the matchbook cover and walked into the cocktail lounge.

A couple of jacketless bartenders were setting up

161

for the lunch crowd and several skimpily dressed waitresses were sitting at a table having coffee.

Benjamin went to the bar and sat down on a stool.

"We're not open yet," one of the bartenders said.

"I'm not here to drink," Benjamin said in his most menacing voice. "I'm here on business."

The two bartenders stopped wiping glasses and looked hard at him.

"Lieutenant Detective Benjamin," he said, answering the question he saw in their faces. He pulled out his wallet and flashed his ID. "Do either of you guys remember seeing these men?" he asked as he put the three-by-five photos of Forbushe and Tull down on the bar. "Better take a look."

The two of them scanned the photos. "This one came in here a few nights a week. Hey, I saw pictures of these guys on TV. They went down in that sub, didn't they?"

"Yeah. Now tell me about him," Benjamin said, pointing to the photograph of Forbushe. "But first tell me your name."

"Eddie."

"Okay, Eddie, now tell me about Lieutenant Commander William Forbushe?"

Eddie shrugged. "A kind of ordinary Joe. I mean, he'd come in here, sit at the bar and have a few drinks—"

"Beer?"

Eddie nodded.

"What about women?"

"He never came here with one, if that's what you mean."

Benjamin stared at Eddie for several moments.

"I never saw him with a broad," Eddie said.

Benjamin's hand shot across the bar and he grabbed ahold of Eddie by the front of his shirt. "You set him up with a hooker?"

Eddie tried to pull away, but Benjamin was stronger and had him bent across the bar in a matter of moments.

"I don't pimp," Eddie said. "Ask anyone." He turned his head toward the other bartender. "Tell him, Murphy, for godsakes tell him."

"He's tellin' the truth," Murphy said.

Benjamin let go of Eddie. "Okay, what did he do for a fuck?"

"I know a guy—he has a string of young ones. Some almost titless. More like boys than girls, if you get my drift."

"I get it. You give me your friend's phone number," Benjamin said.

Eddie shook his head. "He'll have me killed—"

"Write the fucking number down, Eddie," Benjamin said in a hard voice.

Eddie moved over to the cash register, wrote the number down inside of a matchbook cover and then came back to where Benjamin was sitting and handed it to him.

"Good. Now listen to my next question and think before you answer. You listening?"

"Yeah, yeah, I'm listening."

"Did the commander ever come in here with a man?"

Eddie shook his head. "He liked girls who—"

"You already told me that," Benjamin said. "Did he ever meet a male friend here?"

163

"I don't know if they were friends," Eddie said. "But one night he's sitting here, having his usual brew, when this very fat guy walks in and sits down on the stool next to him. Like guys at a bar they begin to talk."

"Did you happen to hear what they were talking about?" Benjamin asked, feeling as if he wanted to jump up and down for joy.

"Hear? Shit, man, I didn't even understand the language they were talking."

Benjamin grinned, slapped the bar and exclaimed, "Eddie, you're a dream boat!" Then he leaned over, pinched his right cheek, got off the stool and, bowing to the waitresses who were still seated at a table, he said cheerily, "And may the fruit of your wombs be as numerous as the stars and bright as the sun." A moment later he was on his way out into the lobby where he headed for the nearest telephone. This time he had two numbers to call. He dialed the pimp's number first. A woman answered and when he told her that Eddie gave him the number because he was looking for something special, she told him to wait a minute and then a man came on, who spoke in a low, soft voice that was almost a whisper. Benjamin arranged to meet him at 12:30 P.M. in front of the East Wind Motel. Then he dialed the number that was inside the matchbook cover he'd found in Forbushe's apartment. This time the line wasn't busy and, after three rings, a woman answered.

"My name is Charles Benjamin," he said, "I'm with the *Norfolk Courier*. I was a friend of—John," he said, using Tull's given name.

She made a small gasping sound.

164

"I know how difficult this is for you," Benjamin said, "but I really would like to meet you."

"How did you get my phone number?"

"John—"

"He wouldn't give my number to another man," she snapped and hung up.

Benjamin put the phone back on the hook and commented aloud, "Why should it be easy, when it can be hard." Then he dialed Headquarters and had the desk sergeant get him the name and address that matched the phone number. The lady was Miss Louise Grant and she lived at 44 Glenwood Road. "Any word from Markham?" he asked.

"None," the desk sergeant answered.

Benjamin thanked him, hung up and a short time later he was standing in front of a brick ranch on a large piece of property, the back of which terminated at the edge of a canal. The day was very hot and humid and, because he was standing in the sun, it seemed a lot hotter. He wiped his brow and the back of his neck with a handkerchief and until he heard someone begin to open the door, he wished he was somewhere else. But the instant the door opened, he knew he was in the right place, at the right time.

"Miss Grant?" Benjamin asked. The woman was beautiful—young, maybe in her mid-thirties. She wore a white terry-cloth bathrobe and from what his experienced eyes could tell, nothing under it.

She nodded.

Benjamin whipped out his wallet and flashed his ID. "Lieutenant Detective Charles Benjamin." He could see she remembered the name and he said,

"You just made it a bit more difficult for me to find you."

She didn't answer.

"I'd like to ask you a few questions about Commander John Tull," he said.

She nodded.

They wound up in the living room. He sat down on the couch, while she settled in a club chair.

"The man's dead," she said, looking straight at Benjamin.

He nodded. "I know this is difficult for you. But for reasons I can't explain, I need to know certain things about Commander Tull."

"We were lovers," she said. "He was a considerate and passionate man."

"Did he ever discuss his work with you?"

"No."

"Did he ever introduce you to his friends?"

Louise shook her head. "He was one of those unique individuals who could enjoy the moment. He never spoke about the past."

"What about the future?" Benjamin asked.

"If you mean did we discuss marriage, that answer is, I wanted to marry him, but—" She stopped and lowered her head.

"I understand," Benjamin said.

She looked up. "Any more questions?"

"No."

They stood up at the same time and she accompanied him back to the door.

"John was a unique man," she said, stepping aside to let him out of the house.

"I don't doubt that for a minute," Benjamin

answered as he stepped into the hot humid air again; then with a smile, he added, "I wish you luck, Miss Grant."

"Stand by at the diving controls," Tull ordered, looking at his watch. It was 1800 local time. Topside the sea would be draped in twilight, with only about fifteen minutes before total darkness would take over. In the deepening twilight, the wake from the periscope and the UHF antenna would be almost impossible to spot, either from the surface or from the air.

"Standing by" came the answer.

"Make periscope depth," Tull said.

"Aye, aye, making periscope depth," the man responded. "Diving planes up five."

Tull felt the bow rise even as he watched the depth gauge. It began from 1500 to move counterclockwise.

"Looking good," the diving control operator said.

They passed through 1200 feet.

Tull moved to the position indicator. The boat would be four hundred miles due west of the Strait of Gibraltar when she came to periscope depth.

"Anything?" he asked, looking over at Haines, who was manning the sonar.

"A tanker heading south, and coaster moving in the opposite direction."

"Eight hundred feet," the diving control operator called.

Tull went to the engine-room telegraph and rang for ahead one third.

A moment later it was answered.

"Five hundred feet," the diving control operator called.

"Periscope depth is fifty-five feet," Tull said, just to be sure the man knew.

Tull checked the board. It was green. His attention went to the depth gauge. They were going through two hundred feet.

"Diving planes moved to zero," the diving control operator said.

The bow dropped slightly, but the boat continued her upward movement.

"One hundred feet," Tull called out.

Suddenly the control room was filled with the sound of hissing air and pumps moving water from one tank to another.

"Forty feet," Tull called, watching the depth gauge. It stopped and started to unwind.

"Periscope depth," Tull said as the needle went to fifty-five feet and held steady.

"Trimmed to the mark," the diving control operator announced with obvious satisfaction.

Tull gave him a thumbs-up and activated the periscope himself. He made a quick 360 sweep. "Nothing," he reported, and lowered the periscope; then he checked the EMS system. "Clear," he said, and raised the UHF antenna.

"A lot of navy traffic," the radio man said.

Forbushe came into the control room.

"High speed stuff . . . algorithmically coded," the radio man said.

Tull didn't even glance at Forbushe. "Send," he told the radio man.

"Sending," the man answered, rapidly moving his fingers over a keyboard until he'd finished typing a thirty-four digit number.

Moments passed.

"Incoming," the radio operator said as a printer suddenly came to life to print a total of fourteen letters.

Tull immediately tore the paper from the printer, stuffed it in his pocket and, lowering the antenna, he called out, "Make five hundred feet."

"Five hundred feet," the man at the diving controls responded.

Tull went to the decoder and, using the monthly code book, correlated the specific groupings of numbers in the message with those in the code book and fed the resulting numbers into the decoder. "Proceed to alternate," Tull said without looking up at Forbushe, who was standing behind him.

"An interesting message," Forbushe said and walked away.

15

"Sir, I picked these two up a few moments ago," a radio man reported to the watch officer in the COMSUBLANT communications center in Norfolk. "This one came from somewhere nearby. I could tell by the strength and the direction of the signal." He handed the officer a printout of fourteen numbers. "The longer one seems almost as if it came from one of the submarines, but none were scheduled to transmit at this time."

The watch officer took the two messages and immediately stamped them top secret and had them hand-carried to the ONI, who had issued a standing order that until further notice all anomalous messages were to be classified as top secret and immediately delivered to the ranking officer on duty.

Captain Walter Exman signed for the two messages and ran the shorter one through the decoder first, wrote the decoded message down, then ran the second, which read, "Sally, Sally . . . Give me your promise . . . Tull."

Exman picked up the phone and punched out a Washington phone number.

"Admiral Corliss," Exman said.

"Who's calling?" the wave on the other end asked.

"Captain Exman."

A moment passed before the admiral identified himself.

"It came," Exman said and clicked off.

Markham visited the agency from which Tull had rented the car. The manager, a short, redheaded man named Horace Coombs complained bitterly that he'd have "to eat the loss of the car."

"I appreciate that," Markham said, sitting opposite him. "I really do, and if there was anything I could do to help you, I would. But I need to know what you know about Commander Tull."

"He paid every month on time, sometimes even early."

"Did he ever come here with anyone?"

"A woman, a real looker."

"You wouldn't happen to know her name, would you?"

Coombs shook his head. "But she was built for action, if you know what I mean."

Markham nodded and, leaving the car rental agency, he drove over to Tull's apartment, which was in a luxury building that had its own swimming pool and health club on the premises.

He had to get the building's manager to unlock the door to the apartment, which he found had a beautiful view of the Chesapeake Bay and was tastefully and expensively furnished. Tull was obviously a reader and had several of the latest fiction and non-fiction books around. He also had a collection of classical CDs, most of which were chamber music.

Markham made a thorough search of the three rooms and the kitchen and bathroom and found nothing.

"Did he ever have anyone visit him that you know of?" Markham asked when he returned to the manager's office.

"Sometimes a woman."

"Could you describe her?"

"Beautiful."

"No male friends?"

"None that I ever saw," the manager answered.

Markham thanked him, got back into the unmarked car and was about to call in to Headquarters and locate Benjamin when he suddenly decided to drive out to the Navy base and speak to the security people over there.

In less than a half hour Markham found himself standing in front of a Marine captain, with the name Mittag on his nametag. "Captain," Markham said, "I want to find out if any of your men saw Commander Tull on the night that *Command One* sailed."

"Is this a civil or military matter?" Mittag asked.

"You can check with the base ONI," Markham said.

Mittag nodded, punched four numbers on the phone, identified himself and then said, "I have a detective here from New York . . . Yes, sir . . . Certainly, sir . . . I'll see to it personally." He put the phone down, called a sergeant and said, "Gunny get me the list of men on duty at *Command One*'s barrier."

Within two minutes, the gunny said, "Privates Sean Gould and Wilber Jones, sir."

"Where are they now?"

"Both men are on duty at gate four, sir," the gunny answered.

Mittag nodded. "I'll take you to gate four myself," he said, looking straight at Markham. "Gunny, I'll be back shortly."

"Yes, sir," the sergeant answered.

Mittag pointed to a jeep.

Five minutes later they pulled up off to the side of the kiosk where two young Marines were monitoring the flow of traffic.

As soon as they saw the lieutenant, they snapped to attention and saluted.

Mittag returned the salute. "The two of you were on duty at the barrier the night *Command One* sailed."

"Yes, sir," they answered almost in unison.

"This man has some questions he wants you to answer," Mittag said, nodding toward Markham.

"Do either of you know Commander Tull?" Markham asked.

"He was the boat's XO," one of them said.

"Did you know him by sight?"

"Yes, sir," one and then the other answered.

"Did you know his car?"

Both men nodded.

"Did anyone ever drive up to the barrier?" Markham asked.

"Yes, sir," they chorused.

Then one said, "A woman."

"What about the night the submarine sailed, did she drive him?"

"No, sir. He was with a man," one of them said.

"A real fat guy," the other commented.

"You're sure about that man being fat?"

"Real sure, you sure, Wilber?" Gould asked.

"Sure, I'm sure," Wilber Smith answered.

"Thank you, men." Markham said; then looking at Mittag, he added, "I don't have any more questions.

The man waiting for Benjamin in front of the motel was tall, slender and well dressed. There was a black Lincoln in the parking lot that was obviously his.

Benjamin parked his car in next to the Lincoln and walked out to where the man was waiting.

"Who gave you my number?" the pimp asked.

"Forbushe, before he left," Benjamin said.

The pimp looked him over, nodded and, offering his hand, he said, "Lucky."

Benjamin shook his hand. "Mostly people call me Chuck."

"I have two women in the car," Lucky said. "One's nineteen, the other twenty-two."

"Which one did Bill take?" Benjamin asked.

Lucky grinned. "As soon as you told me who gave you my number, I knew you'd want the same thing

175

he had. Those two in the car don't fit the bill, but there's something in room ten. About fourteen, doesn't speak much, but knows what to do and how to do it."

Benjamin felt his stomach turn into a huge knot. "Did Bill like her?"

"She was like a drug for him. He wouldn't have anyone else after he had her."

Benjamin nodded.

"But she costs more than the others," Lucky said. "And it's cash up front."

"Let me take a look at her and if she's what you say she is, I'll give your price."

"Two bills," Lucky said.

"No problem," Benjamin answered as they started to walk toward room number ten.

"Sad, about what happened to Bill. He was a good customer," Lucky said. "He even brought me his fat friend. That guy liked a woman with tits and a good ass. You know him?"

"Only in a manner of speaking."

"Has a real sweet tooth, that guy," Lucky commented as he knocked at the door of number ten. "It's me, Lucky, with a friend."

Benjamin could hear the chain removed and then the lock turned.

Lucky smiled at him, turned the knob, opened the door and said, "After you."

Benjamin saw the girl halfway between the door and the opposite wall. She was naked. Her pubes had been shaved.

"Something else, right?" Lucky questioned, closing the door.

176

The girl smiled at him and ran her hand through her short blond hair.

"You just tell her what you want and she'll do it. Isn't that right, Iris?

She nodded.

"Do we have a deal?" Lucky asked.

"Yeah, we have a deal," Benjamin said and, reaching under his jacket, he yanked the .38 free.

Lucky's eyes went wide.

"Move and you'll be a cripple for life," Benjamin said. He moved to the phone, picked it up, asked for an outside line and punched out the number for Headquarters. "Get dressed, Iris," he said before the desk sergeant came on.

"I got four grand in cash," Lucky whined. "You can have it all."

After five rings, the desk sergeant picked up the phone and, before he could say a word, Benjamin told him where he was and what was happening. "Get a couple of uniforms down here," he said and, hanging up, he told Lucky to sit down on one of the two chairs in the room and Iris to do the same on the other. "I want to hear everything you know about Forbushe and the fat man."

"You want to deal?" Lucky asked hopefully.

Benjamin answered with a steely-eyed look. "Talk, Lucky, or you'll go from here to the hospital."

"Iris, you're a witness, you heard him threaten—"

Benjamin crossed the room and backhanded him across the face with the .38.

The blow dropped Lucky to the floor. Blood flowed from a gash on the right side of his face.

Iris started to whimper.

Benjamin reached down and pulled him back into the chair. "I'm not playing fucking games with you," he growled.

Lucky tried to stop the bleeding with a handkerchief.

"Talk," Benjamin said, "or I'll—"

"You tell him, Iris," Lucky said. "I already told you everything I know," he said, looking up at Benjamin.

"He talked crazy languages," Iris said.

"Yeah. Yeah, that's right," Lucky said, "he and the fat man jabbered in . . . in something, I don't know what."

"What else?" Benjamin asked.

"He mainly liked to do it Greek," Iris told him, "but—"

Benjamin waved her silent. "I don't care about that. I want to know if he ever said anything strange."

"Once he said he was a very important man, but no one knew how important."

"Did he ever mention the name John Tull?" Benjamin asked.

Iris grinned and, nodding, she said, "Sure. He hated him. Once just before he shot his load, he started yelling about him. Said he'd like to cut the guy's balls off. It made me laugh so hard that he slipped out of me and shot all over my ass."

Benjamin heard the two squad cars screech to a halt in the parking area, and opening the door, he called out to the uniforms, "There are two in the Lincoln and I have two here."

"That New York detective has been trying to raise

you on the radio, Lieutenant," one of the uniforms said. "I told him where you were and he—"

Another car pulled into the parking lot and stopped.

"Thanks," Benjamin said to the uniform. "That's the New York detective now . . ."

16

Benjamin and Markham were met on the White House lawn where the chopper had landed, and they were escorted directly to the Oval Office to meet the President, the admirals and the directors of the FBI and CIA.

After the introductions, which were made by Hubbered after he introduced Benjamin and Markham to the President, and the handshaking, the President congratulated both of them for—as he put it—"conducting a most meaningful investigation." Then he suggested that they move into a larger conference room, "where we will be joined by Mister Juniper, the Secretary of State, and Mister Hallwick, the Secretary of the Navy."

The movement from the Oval room to one of the conference rooms was accomplished in a matter of minutes. Benjamin was seated on the President's right and Markham on his left.

181

The President looked over at the Secretaries of State and Navy. "I understand Mister Hubbered briefed each of you on the situation," he said.

Both men nodded.

He turned his attention first to Benjamin and then to Markham. "Have you come up with more information that might better help us understand who is behind the theft of *Command One*?"

"Sir," Markham said, "Commander Tull was ID'd with Petrov the night *Command One* sailed. Petrov drove off in the commander's car, the same car that later exploded and killed Petrov."

"So we have an American naval officer linked directly to a KGB agent," the President said, biting the words off as he said them.

"We also have Lieutenant Commander Forbushe linked to the same Russian agent," Benjamin said and explained how he discovered the connection; then he added, "I also know that Forbushe hates Tull and that Petrov and he might have spoken Russian, and another language when they were together."

"And just how did you find that out?" Sykes questioned.

"Through the pimp and the hooker Forbushe patronized," Benjamin answered.

"Just what does Mister Forbushe do aboard the submarine?" the President asked.

"He's the engineering officer," Admiral Hicks answered.

The President shifted in his chair and nodded. "That makes sense," he said. "Tull drives the submarine and Forbushe supplies the power, while the other ten men perform the other tasks necessary to its operation." He stood up and began pacing. "This will have to go down in history as the biggest theft ever." He stopped, pursed his lips and then, moving his hand across his chin, he said, "I think all of us agree that there is no longer any doubt that the May Day from *Command One* was a bogus message and that she is at the moment bound for either Soviet waters or toward a port of some nation even less friendly to us than the Soviets."

"Mister President," the Secretary of State commented, "I have already been told that the Soviets will lodge a formal protest about the number and nature of the ships moving into the waters between the southern tip of Greenland and Ireland."

"Tell them we're looking for one of our submarines," the President said. "I'm sure their people picked up the May Day. We'll play poker with them until we have a better idea about where *Command One* is heading."

The Secretary of State nodded, but he didn't look in the least bit pleased.

"Now, we'll just have to sweat this out," the President said, and returned to his seat. "But in the meantime, there are things that must be done to find out who the agents are in this country, who—"

Admiral Corliss cleared his throat and focused everyone's attention at the table on him. "I have something to reveal that comes under a ten security classification and we do have two nongovernmental people in the room."

183

The President rubbed his chin. "If it wasn't for those 'two nongovernmental people,' as you define them, we wouldn't have a tinker's chance in hell of stopping *Command One* from becoming the property of another nation."

Corliss said, "With all due respect, Mister President, that is not exactly true. The ONI has been aware—"

The President was on his feet. "Are you telling me that you and your people knew that *Command One* would be stolen?" He almost shouted the question.

Corliss's face reddened.

"Admiral, I'm waiting for an answer."

"We knew that something was going to happen, but we didn't know exactly what."

Resting his elbows on the back of the chair, the President said, "Under my specific direction you can share with us the information that in your estimation deserves a number ten priority." His tone was knife-edge sharp.

"Commander Tull is one of our men," Corliss said.

The President gripped the top of the chair so hard that his knuckles turned white before he said, "He is obviously one of theirs too."

"Commander Tull is a double agent," Corliss said.

"By Christ, I don't believe what I'm hearing!" the President exclaimed. This time he did shout.

"He is and has been—"

"Ten men have been killed—no, fourteen, including the officer on the submarine and those men in the

184

chopper. Just what the hell do you think you've been running?"

Corliss, his face still very red, answered, "Two hours ago Tull transmitted a message from *Command One*."

"Can you tell me where that submarine is, Admiral?" the President demanded.

"I can only tell you that Commander Tull's mission is to foil the hijacking."

"One man against ten?" the President questioned in a controlled fury.

"We have two additional men on board," Corliss said.

"I suppose they too are double agents?"

Corliss nodded. "They notified us that they were given papers and told to report aboard the *C-1* and to ID themselves to Commander Tull by each presenting him with a piece of puzzle. At the time they notified us, we still had no idea that they were taking the place of two regularly assigned crewmen."

"And no one thought to check their assignment?"

"No, Mister President," Corliss answered forthrightly. "But I'm sure that if a check would have been made, it would not have indicated anything unusual. The unusual was Commander Tull's assignment and when we checked that, it showed no irregularities."

"So now the numbers are three against seven," the President responded sarcastically.

Corliss poured himself a glass of water from the carafe in front of him and with a steady hand lifted it to his mouth and drank most of it before he said, "Mister President, if you request it, after I explain the situation, the Secretary of the Navy will have my resignation on his desk by nine o'clock tomorrow morning." He put the glass down.

"We are all ready to listen to you," the President said, resuming his seat.

"My office has been aware for some time that something was going to happen to *Command One*. We got bits and pieces of this from various sources almost from the first moment she was conceived. Naturally, we didn't know exactly what. Then six months ago Commander Tull notified us that he was being transferred from his regular assignment aboard a boomer to the *C-1,* even the C-1's skipper, Captain Smith, had requested his former XO. Practically all such requests are granted by BUPERS; therefore, when this one wasn't and one of our men was substituted, we were sure that the Russians were involved."

"Is Forbushe one of your men?"

"No, he is not. But Commander Tull reported to us that he would have a major role in whatever was going to happen. Tull's contact, namely, Petrov, had no idea of what was really being planned."

"Tull was responsible for Petrov's death, then?"

"Yes, Mister President, and probably the death of the officer aboard the *C-1* and the destruction of the chopper."

"Quite a man, this double agent Tull of yours," the President commented dryly.

"Excuse me, Admiral," Benjamin said, "but it seems impossible that Tull didn't know the *C-1* would be hijacked."

"Yes, you're probably right," Corliss answered.

"If he knew," the President jumped in, "why didn't he notify you immediately."

"Agents, Mister President, are not like the rest of us, especially someone like Commander Tull. I can not tell why he didn't inform us, but I can tell you that he is completely loyal and—"

A knock at the door stopped Corliss from finishing his statement.

Hubbered nodded to the President, left the table and answered the door.

"For Admiral Corliss," a Marine captain said, handing Hubbered a sealed envelope.

Hubbered returned to the table and handed the envelope to Corliss.

"Please excuse me for a few moments, gentlemen," Corliss said, opening the envelope and removing the flimsy paper. After a moment of reading it, he smiled. "Mister President, radio operator on the aircraft carrier *America* picked up the radio transmission from the *C-1* and was able to get an approximate fix on it. At the time it was transmitted it was between four and five hundred miles west of the *America*'s position and she was just clearing the Strait of Gibraltar and on a course due west to take up her position at the entrance to the strait."

The President nodded. "Who says the world doesn't turn on luck," he commented. "But that still doesn't tell us where she's going, does it?"

"The *America* and several destroyers are already steaming toward the area where she was located," Corliss said.

"Continue with your explanation," the President told him.

"We did not know that ten members of the crew would be murdered and replaced."

"Correct me if I'm wrong," the President said. "You're telling me that the unknowns in all of this are Forbushe and seven other men."

"Yes," Corliss answered. "My guess is that Tull is trying to figure out who's running Forbushe."

"Obviously the Russians are," Sykes, the director of the CIA said.

"Tull wasn't sure," Corliss answered.

"You mean that man could be a triple agent?" the Secretary of the Navy asked.

"He could be," Corliss answered. "I don't know. But I haven't finished, Mister President."

"Please continue."

"The May Day and the fact that it was sent only once from an area of the ocean that is more than three miles deep leads me to believe, that the *C-1* went down as a result of sabotage. Then detectives Benjamin and Markham became involved . . . after that you know the sequence of events."

"We'll discuss the matter of your resignation another time," the President said. "Now we must focus all our efforts at finding those people connected with this and finding the *C-1*." He looked at Corliss. "There's no guarantee that Tull will make it out of this alive, or for that matter anyone."

"Does your order to fire on her still stand?" Admiral Hicks asked.

"No, give her a chance. If she fails to respond to a signal to immediately surface and stop, then destroy her."

17

Tull, immediately after receiving the message, had resumed a northward course at a speed of forty knots and now, two hours later, as he made a routine inspection of the engine room, he was still trying to understand its meaning. There wasn't any alternate destination. The plan was to sail the *C-1* as close as possible to Russian territorial waters and then, if nothing else happened, make a mistake that would enable an American ship to capture them. Tull had always been certain that Forbushe wouldn't have the stomach to risk being sunk. It was one thing to play games during a deep dive when he was in control of the situation, but it would be something else again, to take fire . . .

Tull just about reached the control room when he suddenly realized that Forbushe understood the message and had been playing a cat-and-mouse game with him . . . a game that he too could play with great skill. He continued to the control room, switched on the 1MC and said, "Now hear this . . . All hands now hear this . . . We're going to periscope depth . . . We're going to periscope depth." Then, switching off the 1MC, he looked back over his shoulder at the diving control operator, "Make periscope depth, five five feet."

"Diving plane up five. Setting for five five feet," the operator answered.

The *C-1*'s bow began to lift and, automatically, a sequenced opening and closing of air and seawater valves changed the amount of water in the ballast tanks, making the *C-1* more buoyant.

Forbushe came racing into the control room.

"I decided to check that message," Tull said.

Forbushe shook his head. "Not necessary," he said. "Absolutely not necessary."

"Then you understood it?" Tull asked. They had already gone up two hundred feet. He had to go to five hundred before he'd belay his previous command.

"I was just waiting to see how long it would take you to—"

"To go to you and ask if you knew what it meant?"

Forbushe managed a smile.

"Not funny," Tull said starkly. "Not in the least bit fucking funny." He checked the depth gauge: it was winding back rapidly. "Level at five hundred," he barked.

"Level at five hundred," the diving control operator said. "Diving planes moved to zero."

Tull checked the board. It was green.

"Five hundred feet," the diving control operator said. "Trimmed to the mark."

Tull motioned to one of the men. "Take the conn," he said. "I'll be in my cabin with Mister Forbushe. Any change to operating status, let me know immediately."

"Yes, sir," the man answered.

Moments later they entered Tull's cabin and Tull closed the door behind them. "Okay, what's the alternate destination?"

"Tripoli."

Tull stopped his jaw from going slack. The first shoe had just been dropped, but he had to pretend he hadn't been waiting for it to happen, or to have heard its silent ominous thud. "That was prearranged between you and—"

"People higher than Harry," Forbushe cut in.

Tull wondered if Forbushe knew that Harry had become history?

"You know that frequently the vital information isn't given to one man," Forbushe said.

Tull nodded. "If I didn't know it before, I know it now," he commented.

"The delivery is made in Tripoli," Forbushe said, almost airily. "We get paid off there and the Russians will sail her, under a Russian flag, to Odessa."

"Under a Russian flag?"

"That's the beauty of the scheme," Forbushe said. "If an American ship attacks it, it will be considered an act of war."

193

"Whoever thought that one up—" Tull smiled. "We'll just glide through the Strait of Gibraltar and Libya, here we come."

"If we change course now and maintain forty knots, we should be at the Strait in a little over twelve hours. It will be easy to enter the Med under the protective sound of any large tanker. Even a good-size cruise ship would give us the covering sound we need."

Tull realized that Forbushe had been doing a lot of homework, as the expression goes, at least a great deal of thinking about where the *C-1* was and where he wanted it to go.

"Come to course one hundred and thirty degrees and we'll be on a straight line to the Strait."

Tull smiled. He was totally aware that Forbushe had just given him an order and, if he obeyed, Forbushe would become the skipper of the *C-1*, but given the situation, he didn't see any way he could refuse. "The Strait," he said and, switching on the 1MC, he said, "Helmsman, come to course one hundred and thirty degrees."

Forbushe offered his hand. "Let bygones be bygones."

Tull shook it. "Absolutely. But I do have a question. What will happen to the crew when we reach port?"

Forbushe shrugged. "That's not our concern." He flashed a big smile. "Each of us will be several million dollars richer."

Tull answered Forbushe's smile with one of his own, but said nothing.

"I'm going back to the control room," Forbushe said.

Tull nodded. What Forbushe was really saying was that he'd take the conn until they'd get through the straits. But ten hours was a long long time.

Forty hours after *Command One* sent its May Day, the aircraft carrier *America*, an eighty-three-thousand-ton monster with the capability in its fighter and bomber wings of inflicting enormous damage on either a fleet of enemy ships, land-based targets or destroying aircraft in the sky, was steaming west through the night-covered sea, screened by two destroyers, the *William Penn* and the *Charles Bains*, and two guided missile frigates, the *Mitscher* and the *Frank Knox*. The *Penn* and the *Bains* were two thousand yards off the *America*'s port and starb'd bows, respectively, while the *Frank Knox* and *Penn* steamed a thousand yards astern of the carrier, almost in the wakes of the two destroyers. Making thirty knots, the carrier battle group maintained a Condition 2, or modified general quarters.

Commander Richard Pierce manned the command desk in the Combat Decision Center, an air-conditioned space several levels below the flight deck, where information about every vessel above and below the sea—or every aircraft picked up by its own search radars, or by its screen or by the two E-2C Hawkeye, early-warning defensive aircraft flying in patterns five hundred miles from the carrier—was monitored and displayed on several huge screens.

"Everything out there," Pierce said, "should be out there." Hailing from Indian Head, South Dakota, and a Sioux Indian on his mother's side, he had a characteristic western drawl.

The officer to whom he spoke, Lieutenant Jay Crisp, was a tall thin black man from New York. He had the mid-watch at the command desk. "Two Hawkeyes up and Sea King, chopper being readied to take off," he said, looking at the electronic status board that indicated the type of aircraft airborne and those that were being readied for airborne operations. The Sea King, the SH-3H, was a gas-driven helicopter, equipped with state-of-the-art ASW capabilities.

"The chopper came up on board about five minutes ago," Pierce said. "I checked with flight Ops and was told that the skipper wants it out."

Crisp laughed. "An' what the skipper wants, he gets. Man, when I get to command one of these babies, I'm going to want me one hell of a lot of things."

Pierce nodded. "But by that time, you'll be too damn old to enjoy them."

They both laughed, then Pierce asked, "You know what this is all about—I mean why we left the Med."

"Beats the shit out of me," Crisp said. "But I caught some conversation between the XO and the CAG. Seems we're looking for a submarine."

"Ours?"

196

Crisp shrugged and looked at the clock. "About that time," he said and recited, "I am ready to relieve you, sir."

Pierce stood up and stretched. There was no particular information he had to pass on to Crisp.

"I relieve you," Crisp said and took his place at the command desk.

Directly in back of the command desk, where secondary radar scopes were located and at the far side, where the sonar station was, the men for mid-watch were changing places with those who had the first watch.

"It must be theirs—the sub, I mean," Crisp commented, "or we wouldn't be on Condition Two."

"I'm going to get a sandwich and coffee," Pierce said. "I don't know why, but I'm hungry."

"Tension," Crisp said. "Tension."

Suddenly a light on the aircraft operational status board began to blink.

Crisp picked up one of the two dozen phones and was immediately connected to the signal bridge. "CDC, you launching that Sea King?"

"Gone," the voice on the other end reported.

"Roger," Crisp answered. The status board indicated that the chopper was airborne. He gave his attention back to Pierce. "The best way to get rid of tension—" he grinned "—besides a good roll in the sack, is to do yoga exercises, and since you can't get a roll in the sack on board, then yoga exercises are the next best thing."

Pierce made a face and left the CDC. Tension always gave him an appetite.

Benjamin was awake, even though it was 2 A.M. Liz was sleeping next to him, her breath regular and slow. Being with her again was a profound emotional experience. He had discovered just how much he loved her and just how lonely he had been. Lying there, with her close, he decided that he would buy a house—they had one before the divorce—on the bay and maybe give some serious thought to what he'd like to do when he retired. He'd soon have the requisite twenty-five years in and, though he wouldn't get his pension until he was fifty-five, he could start a new career. Liz would certainly be happier if he could find some other line of work. There were other things he often thought he'd like to do, or at least try. He loved photography and was getting good at it. Becoming a professional photographer had been something that he had thought about from time to time. He had also thought about running a charter fishing boat. That kind of life appealed to him.

He looked at Liz again and smiled. She had asked him what his day had been like and all he said was, "Different, very different from most days."

She hadn't pressed him to be more explicit and he was grateful for that. Eventually, he'd explain as much as he could about it without touching on the security aspects of it. But he'd have to do it in his own way, in his own time . . . and bit by bit.

Earlier in the evening, he and Markham had been

flown by chopper back to the air base and then had been driven home in a Navy staff car, dropping Markham off first at the motel. The day had been charged with excitement and, though he had taken everything in stride while it had been happening, now in the middle of the night, he found himself fully charged and unable to fall asleep again.

Carefully leaving the bed, lest he wake Liz, Benjamin tiptoed out of the bedroom and made his way through the darkened apartment to the kitchen, where, in the still-darkened room, he went to the closet above the sink, where he kept a bottle of Glenlivet and took it down. He opened it, poured a good three fingers into an ordinary water glass and was about to open the refrigerator's freezer compartment and take an ice cube tray out when a car moving slowly up the street, caused the dog in the ground-floor apartment opposite his to begin barking.

"You tell them, Dimitri," Benjamin said aloud, as if he were talking to the dog. "You tell them, boy." But even as he spoke, he suddenly realized that he and the car had passed the window at the same time and the car hadn't any lights on. For a moment, he hesitated; then he shouted, "Liz . . . Liz!" And running back into the bedroom, he grabbed hold of her feet and pulling her off the bed, he threw himself on top of her.

The next instant something came crashing through the window.

Benjamin scrambled to his feet, dragged Liz to hers and got the two of them through the door when, with a tremendous roar, one side of the bedroom exploded into a raging fire that fell, like a rampaging waterfall, over the bed.

"Oh my God!" Liz screamed.

"Let's get the hell out of here," he said, moving her toward the front of the apartment, where from a hall closet he took two light coats for them and then left the apartment.

The other people in the building streamed out of it, and by the time the fire trucks arrived, the fire had destroyed most of Benjamin's apartment and was eating its way to the second floor and across the hall.

Benjamin led Liz to the chief's car, identified himself and asked if he could use the car's radio telephone.

"Sure, Lieutenant," the chief answered.

Benjamin called Markham. "Get your asses out of there," he said. "I've just been firebombed."

"You and Liz—"

"We're okay," Benjamin said. "Get out now. Don't check out, leave through the service entrance and walk down the street to the next motel. I'll call Headquarters and have a squad car pick the two of you up, then we'll figure out what to do."

"Payback?" Markham responded.

"Yeah, probably," Benjamin said. "Now get your asses out of there." He clicked off and then put through a call to the police department and explained what just had happened to the captain on duty. "I'm going to need clothes for me and my wife, a squad car and a driver," he said.

"Clothes for you won't be a problem," the captain said. "But getting clothes for your wife—"

"Call a couple of the married guys and see what you can come up with. She needs some, even if it's just jeans and a shirt," Benjamin said and put the phone down.

"Did I hear right when I heard you say you were firebombed?" the chief asked.

"It came in through the window," Benjamin said, pointing to the fire-charred opening that now looked like a large, ugly gouged-out eye.

"Any idea who did it?"

Benjamin shook his head. "Not by name, but when I find them, well—" he looked at Liz, smiled and said, "I don't like my sleep being disturbed."

She smiled too and added, "And I was having such a wonderful dream."

He wrapped his arm around hers. "You'll have to tell it to me," he said, almost as if the fire chief wasn't there.

"I will," Liz answered. "I will even demonstrate parts of it to you, and that's a promise . . ."

The phone on the night table next to the President's bed rang and Hubbered said, "Mister President, there is increased Russian submarine activity immediately off our coast—"

"How far off our coast?"

"At the two-hundred-mile range," Hubbered answered. "But that certainly is well within missile-striking range of our major cities from Chicago and St. Louis east to the Coast."

"How many submarines?"

"Four of their Delta 3s."

"Can we track them at all times?"

"Yes, Mister President."

"Can we make it very apparent that we will fire at them the instant they make any attempt to launch?"

"I have been told by the CNO that we must be the ones to fire first. It will be too late to stop them from launching their missiles if we wait until—"

"I get the picture," the President said.

"There's more, Mister President," Hubbered said.

"I'm listening."

"Several attack-type submarines are headed in the direction of *C-1*. It's obvious the Russians too had received the signal from *C-1*. Our people believe that attack submarines will be used to escort *C-1* through our blockade."

The President was sitting up now, resting against the bed's headboard. "How far is the *America* from *C-1*'s last estimated position?" he asked, knowing that Hubbered would have obtained that before he phoned him.

"Two hundred and fifty nautical miles."

Looking at a nearby digital clock, the President said, "It's 2:30. Have the various Chiefs of Staff, the secretaries of Defense, the Army and Navy, and my Secretary of State in the war room by 4 A.M."

"Yes, Mister President."

"And arrange a direct radio phone link with the skipper of the *America*. Make sure it's scrambled, though."

"I have already seen to it, Mister President," Hubbered answered.

"Thanks, Brett," the President said. "Having you around here makes my life a bit easier." He put the phone down and realized his wife was awake and looking up at him. "It's very serious" was all he said, as he left the bed and went toward the bathroom for a quick shower.

18

"Let's look at what we have," the President said, looking straight at Steven Fletcher, the CNO. "We have four Russian missile-carrying subs off our east coast and we have ordered four of our boomers to take up positions off the Russian north coast in the Arctic and four more off their Pacific coast."

"Mister President, their attack submarines, six, at last count, I believe, are on a collision course with the *America*'s battle group."

"If push comes to shove, can they handle them?"

"Yes, but that means allowing the *C-1* the possibility of escaping," the admiral said.

"Unacceptable!" the President snapped. "That submarine must not fall into Russian hands."

"Mister President," Admiral Fletcher said, "as she moves north, her area of operation narrows. She must go through—"

"The Russians will be there with more submarines and surface ships," the President said. "We would be playing it very close to the vest to allow that

205

submarine to get anywhere near a large Russian force." Then, turning to Hubbered, who was seated on his right, he said, "I want to speak to the skipper of the *America*."

"His name is Roger Maylee," Hubbered said. "I'll have him on the line in a moment."

The President studied the huge electronic situation board. The position of every American and Russian vessel was clearly indicated. Red squares for the Russian ships, each with a letter designation to indicate the type of ship, and blue squares for the American ships with the same letter designations used for the Russians. Aircraft were indicated with wings: red for theirs, blue for ours and type differentiated by letter.

"They certainly outnumber us in submarines," he commented more to himself than to any of the men at the table. "But we have more carriers and destroyer types at sea." He turned to the Air Force General Carl Krantz, a member of the Joint Chiefs of Staff, and said, "Put everything SAC has in the air. I want the Russians to see those planes—"

"But that will make it possible for them to attack them—"

"Put them in the air, General," the President snapped.

"Captain Maylee is on, Mister President," Hubbered said.

The President took the phone and said, "Captain Maylee, there are six Russian attack submarines heading your way. The best thinking here says that they will escort *C-1* to one of their ports. I want you to prevent . . . I don't want you to fire on those

206

Russian submarines, but you have my permission to fire on and if necessary destroy the *C-1*."

"Yes, sir, I understand that," Maylee answered.

"Captain, in the event that any of the Russian submarines make a hostile move, I do not want to put your ship or any of your escort ships at risk."

"Yes, sir, I understand that too."

"What you and your men do out there, Captain, may well determine what happens to the rest of the world. Do you have any questions?"

"If the situation arises where I must fire on a Russian craft, do I need your permission, or am I free to exercise my own judgment?"

"Captain Maylee, I rely completely on your judgment," the President responded. "But before you fire, take a few moments to think about the way Hiroshima and Nagasaki looked after they had been bombed with the atomic bomb; then take another moment to envision what would happen to our cities and theirs with the kinds of weapons we now have."

There was a pause before Captain Maylee said, "I have a family, Mister President."

The President nodded. "Come see me when this is all over, Captain. I'll introduce your family to mine."

"It would be a pleasure, Mister President."

"Good luck, Captain," the President said and put the phone down. "A good man," he said, clearing his throat. "A good man." Then, turning his attention back to the Air Force General, he said, "We're going to go to the brink with this one, let's hope we don't go over it."

"Mister President, the press is beginning to get

wind that something big is taking place," the Secretary of State told him. "I don't think we can keep this buttoned up much longer."

"How much longer do you think we can go without an explanation?"

"By tonight the latest."

"Alright, arrange for me to go on the air at eight tonight," the President said. "If it's settled by then, I'll have something to report that should make everyone happy. If it's not—well, I think everyone in the country at least should know where they stand."

"Yes, Mister President," the Secretary of State answered.

That Forbushe didn't leave the control room, Tull knew, was obvious to the men, and that the course had been changed from a northward run to a southeasterly one common knowledge. But he continued to pretend that nothing unusual had happened. He stood his watch and made the various checks of the instruments that he had done in the past. Then as he and Haines left the control room together, Tull said, "My cabin now." It was a gambit that he would have had to take sooner or later, and he was beginning to feel the enormous pressure of his situation.

As soon as they were behind a closed door, Tull said, "I want a straight answer, Haines, about you and Moussarakis."

"Shoot?"

"How far will the two of you back me?"

Haines smiled. "That's why we're here," he said.

Tull offered him a cigarette from the pack on his desk and took one himself. "We're going the wrong way to the wrong place," Tull said, blowing smoke out of his nose."

Haines nodded and blew a couple of smoke rings.

"In a few hours we're going to have problems," Tull said. "By now, every fucking ship in two navies must be searching for us and one of them is going to find us."

"Ten men can't handle this boat in a combat situation," Haines said. "It's just about wearing the ten of us thin just operating her now."

"I'm going to reactivate part of the crew," Tull said.

"You can do that?" Haines questioned with wonderment.

Tull snapped his fingers. "Not quite like that, but damn close to it. But I'm not going to do it until Forbushe has run himself down and we're in trouble. I want trouble inside as well as outside. I'll cause the trouble inside."

"You mean you want to take over the boat?"

Tull nodded. "Either before we have to get into a fight with whoever finds us, or while we're trying to avoid being sunk."

"Sunk?"

"It's a real possibility," Tull said. "We're going the wrong way, and that's going to confuse the hell out of everyone, and confused people are apt not to see all the options. Pass the word to Moussarakis to stay alert."

"Aye, aye sir," Haines responded. "Anything else?"

"If you have a rabbit's foot, or any other talisman, start rubbing it," Tull said.

Haines stepped out of the cabin, leaving Tull alone. He waited a few minutes; then he too left and headed directly to the captain's cabin, where, in addition to the captain, the diving officer and the sonar officer had been moved shortly before Forbushe had ordered a course change.

The captain was in his bunk, as he had been since becoming ill. The other two officers were in canvas cots.

Hacker, the sonar officer, was out of it. Howard, the diving officer, was in better shape, and the captain was asleep.

Tull bent over Howard. "Do you hear me?"

"Yes," Howard answered weakly.

"Listen carefully to what I tell you," Tull said, "and as soon as the captain wakes, tell him what I told you. Do you understand?"

"I understand."

"I am not what you think I am," Tull said. "I am with the ONI and in a short time I will need the three of you to help me. Do you understand what I just said?"

Hacker whispered, "Yes."

"Remember," Tull said, "I'm with ONI."

Hacker closed his eyes; he took a deep breath and with a ragged exhalation was asleep.

Sweating, Tull stood up. He'd wait awhile longer before taking matters in his own hands and—

"Don't believe you," Smith croaked from behind him.

Tull turned. The captain had feigned sleep; he had

210

heard everything. "We're headed for Tripoli," Tull said, squatting down alongside the man's bunk.

Smith's lips quivered before he repeated, "Tripoli."

"Listen to me," Tull said, "we're going to run into some heavy action very soon. I can't handle the boat with the crew I have. I need you, Hacker and Howard. Maybe some of the other men too. There's no way we're going to make it without your help."

"Then what?"

"You'll just have to trust me," Tull said.

Smith shook his head.

Tull realized there was no way in hell that he'd get Smith to change his mind and if he didn't, neither would Hacker or Howard. And he needed the three of them. "Alright, you play it any way you want to," he said, "but I'm going to give you and those two a shot at keeping yourselves and the rest of the crew alive. What you do with that chance is up to you. But my advice to you is to continue to act sick until I come for you, or send someone for you."

"And if you can't do that?" Smith asked.

"Then, Skipper," Tull said with a tired smile, "then we're all fish bait. Think it over." And he quickly injected the three men with the antitoxin. "Twenty minutes from now, you'll be perfectly normal," Tull told him and he left the cabin.

19

The Sea King was making a final sweep a hundred and fifty miles in front of the *America* before returning to its flight deck, when its ASW officer, Lieutenant (jg) Paul Fergison saw the change on the magnetic anomaly detector, the device that indicated minute changes in the strength of the earth's magnetic field—shifts that tell an experienced operator he's located an enemy submarine or a metal wreck that has been on the bottom of the sea for years.

"Skip, I just a got a real big spike," Fergison reported over the radio to the pilot, Lieutenant Van Ridder. "Make a three sixty."

"Got enough juice for one more pass and then home," Ridder answered, already bringing the chopper around.

"Come in right over the deck," Fergison said. "That spike has moved some." And he dropped a sonar buoy that started transmitting the moment it hit the water. "Positive contact!" Fergison shouted.

"Positive contact."

"You sure now?" Ridder questioned.

"Give me our position."

Ridder called out the latitude and longitude that was indicated on the navigational computer.

"I make her to be fifteen hundred feet down, on a one three five heading," Fergison advised.

"I'll radio it in," Ridder said and, banking around her, headed back to the carrier.

"This *Blue King One*, calling Blue Base," Ridder's voice came in sharp and clear over the PA system in *America*'s CDC.

Crip's eyes immediately went to one of the three large display screens in front of him, while he moved certain switches that placed him in direct radio contact with the chopper's pilot. "I read you loud and clear *Blue King One*." Even as he spoke, he pressed a series of buttons that changed the definition of the center screen and placed the chopper in exact position relative to the carrier and true north.

"We have a positive," Ridder said, giving the latitude and longitude."

"Depth?"

"Fifteen hundred feet."

"Heading?"

"One three fiver," Ridder answered.

Crisp punched in all of the data he'd just gotten into a target selector computer and immediately that data came up on the display screen at the indicated latitude and longitude and with it appeared a choice of various weapon systems.

"Low on juice," Ridder said. "Comin' home to roost, Blue Base. ETA twenty-five minutes."

"Roger, come on home, *Blue King One*," Crisp answered.

One of the phones on the command desk rang. Reaching for it, Crisp knew it was the skipper.

"Got all of it on the bridge," Maylee said. "We'll be launching another chopper to go out there and get us some more data."

"Aye, aye, sir," Crisp responded.

"We're going to Condition One," Maylee said and, the next instant, the klaxon began to scream and was immediately followed by the skipper announcing over the 1MC, "Now hear this . . . All hands now hear this . . . This is the captain speaking . . . All hands, battle stations . . . All hands, battle stations."

Crisp checked the electronic status board. The second Sea King was already aloft. . . .

Tull returned to the control room to find Forbushe peering intently at the sonar display scope and at the same time adjusting an auxiliary set of headphones on his head.

"I don't know what the hell it is," the man grumbled.

Forbushe shook his head and, slipping the earphones above his ears, he answered, "I don't hear anything and there's nothing on the scope."

"There was something there a few minutes ago," the man grumbled.

Forbushe looked over to where Tull was standing. "You want to listen?" he asked.

Tull nodded and moved over to where the sonar display was.

Forbushe took off the headphones and handed them to him.

Tull realized that he had just been handed a new poker hand. He put the headset on and listened and didn't hear anything except the usual sounds made by the creatures of the sea. But he reached down and increased the amplification, then toyed with the electronic filters.

"What is it?" Forbushe asked anxiously.

Feigning intense concentration, Tull didn't answer.

"What the hell is it?" Forbushe demanded.

Tull looked at him. "Want my best guess?" he asked, taking off the headset and holding it.

"Best guess," Forbushe nodded.

"A sonar buoy," Tull said, saying the first thing that came into his mind that would rattle Forbushe. "But that's a guess. I'm really not sure. The only way to be sure from now on about what we pick up is to have an expert monitoring the gear."

Forbushe squinted at him. "What do you mean?"

Tull handed the headphones back to him. "I'm no expert, that's for sure." And he walked away.

Still holding the headphones in his hand, Forbushe followed him. "Just what the hell did you mean by 'to be really sure from now on?'"

"You really didn't think that we'd be able to pull this off without a problem?"

"The Russians are waiting for us up north. We're

216

heading southeast—"

Tull held up his hand. "You knew what the score was when you changed course. We're supposed to be someplace and we're not. I radioed a prearranged signal and we received an answer. That answer had to have been monitored by the Russians and certainly by the Americans too. You didn't really think either of them wouldn't try to stop us. My guess is that both are searching for us."

Forbushe studied him for several long moments before he said, "This boat will be brought safely to Tripoli."

"If it's not, then we're all dead," Tull answered. "But my suggestion to you, given the fact that the sonar buoy probably transmitted our position—"

Forbushe ran his hand over his face.

"The truth is, Bill," Tull said, using Forbushe's given name to accentuate his sincerity, "if we really do become involved in any sort of an encounter with either the Russians or the Americans we can't handle it with the men we have. We have just enough men to operate the boat, nothing more, and all of us are beginning to be very tired, and tired men make mistakes. A mistake under fifteen hundred feet of water could prove to be absolutely fatal."

Forbushe took several deep breaths.

"We need Hacker, Howard and the skipper," Tull said, and before Forbushe could question him about Smith, he said, "Even if it means holding him at gunpoint to get him to do what you want. If you don't use him, you won't be able to use the other two. But if he does what you want, even at gunpoint, then the others will do it too." Tull stopped; he'd run out of things to say.

"Alright, get the three of them," Forbushe said.

Benjamin and Markham took Liz and Karin to a motel in Franklin, a small town west of Virginia Beach, and by 7:30 in the morning they were sipping coffee from a container at Benjamin's desk at the police station.

Neither one was in much of a mood to talk, and when one of the other detectives mentioned that the President was planning to speak to the nation on the radio that night, Benjamin accepted the news without comment and Markham responded with a very flat, "That's interesting."

Then the detective said, "Speaking about 'interesting,' did either of you guys know that the pimp you busted was an illegal alien from Libya?"

Benjamin was on his feet so fast he forgot to move back and slammed both his knees against the underside of the desktop and Markham practically dropped the container of coffee he was holding.

"You sure?" Benjamin asked, falling back into his chair and rubbing both his knees.

"Yeah."

"Where is he?" Markham asked.

"Some high-powered lawyer named Karl Lotz came down from Washington and got him out and took full responsibility for him."

"Any priors?"

The detective shook his head. "Just a pimp. Been in this country two, three years and has been a pimp practically all that time."

"You have an address for this Karl Lotz?" Benjamin asked.

"It's on the signout sheet," the detective answered.

"Yeah, that's real interesting," Benjamin said; then looking at Markham, he added, "I'll be ready to move just as soon as I finish my coffee, what about you?"

Markham nodded.

"Let's pay Eddie the bartender a visit first," Benjamin said. "This time I think a home visit will be more effective."

"You have an address?"

"Yeah, his full name is Edward Drexel. He lives in Norfolk. Twenty-four Twenty Dockside Road, apartment three A," Benjamin said, reading the information off an index card he'd taken out of his desk.

"I don't remember you getting all that," Markham commented.

With his eyes twinkling, Benjamin said, "I did it when you weren't looking."

The President stood by the window in the Oval Office and looked at the rose garden. He had been working on the speech he would deliver to the nation that night and found that he was having enormous difficulty finding the words that would explain why the country and the Soviet Union were on the brink of starting a war with each other, a war that might come at any moment—perhaps even before he had time to deliver the speech—and kill millions of people and end civilization on the planet as we know it. He had small children of his own, whom he hoped to see grow into worthwhile human beings and—

A soft knock at the door made him turn from the window. "Come in," he called out.

Hubbered entered and quickly closed the door behind him. "The *America* has located a submarine, Mister President. One of their choppers found it a short while ago."

The President stepped away from the window. "Theirs or ours?" he asked.

"It has not been identified," Hubbered said.

The President gestured to the chair in front of his desk and said, "Sit down, Brett." But he continued to stand, resting the arms on the back of his chair. "You know what the stakes are, and I've been standing here trying to think of the right way—if there's a right way—to tell the people of this country that it could all be over before the night is out."

Hubbered nodded. "It's an awesome responsibility."

The President answered with a nod of his own. "I didn't think it could happen during my administration. In the sixties there was the Bay of Pigs and the Cuban Missile Crisis; then President Carter had the Hostage Crisis and Reagan the Iran-Contra business and I have this. If we survive, the one thing I promise you is there will be no more operations like the one run by ONI. No more operations that can put us in the midst of nuclear war."

"Are you going to ask for Admiral Corliss's resignation?"

The President shook his head. "That would be like closing the door after the horse ran out. No, this is something we could all learn from. But there must be safeguards in place to prevent this kind of thing from ever happening again."

"If the people on the Hill get wind of this—"

"They will, you can be sure they will, and there probably will be an investigation. But we'll do them one better, we'll broadly hint that the *C-1* was on a special mission to the Persian Gulf and successfully completed it, but because it would violate our national security interests, we cannot give out any more information."

"What about the men on board—that is, if they survive?"

"No one would believe that they were hijacked— it's too incredible a story, I still have trouble believing it," the President said.

"It won't really wash with the people on the Hill," Hubbered told him frankly.

"I know it won't," the President answered with a slight twinkle in his blue eyes. "But it sure will obfuscate the issue, won't it?"

"Yes, Mister President, it certainly will do that," Hubbered agreed with ever so slight a smile on his lips.

"Good, then we'll do it," the President said; then he added, "And thanks, Brett, for still being able to share a smile with me."

"My pleasure, Mister President," Brett said and, sensing that the President wanted to return to his speech-writing, he stood up and walked quietly and quickly out of the office.

20

Benjamin and Markham drove to within a block of where Eddie lived and walked the rest of the way, aware that most of the people they passed had enough familiarity with the police to make them. The neighborhood was down at the heels and the building, a two-story wooden structure with garbage cans outside, empty beer bottles on the steps and a hallway that smelled.

"Three A," Benjamin said.

Markham nodded, drew his .38 and snapped the safety off.

Benjamin already had his out. Nodding, he whispered, "We'll try it the easy way first." And he knocked on the door.

No answer.

Benjamin knocked again, this time more forcefully.

"Okay, okay," Eddie called out. "Hold your fucking horses!"

"Sounds pissed," Markham commented in a whisper.

"Wait till he finds out who's been knocking on his door," Benjamin answered with a smile and, hearing Eddie approach the door, he said, "Open up, Eddie, it's Detective Benjamin."

From behind the door, there was a momentary cessation of movement.

"Do it easy, Eddie," Benjamin said, "or there won't be much of the door left."

The lock snapped open.

Benjamin nodded to Markham, who turned the knob and pushed the door open with his right foot, while holding the .38 at ready.

Eddie was wearing blue Jockey shorts and no T-shirt. His muddy green eyes went from Markham to Benjamin.

Past Eddie was the bedroom. There was a nude woman in the bed.

"Cops," Eddie snarled, glancing back toward the woman. "Shit, can't a guy get laid without—"

Benjamin recognized the woman. She was one of the waitresses having coffee when he'd visited Eddie at the motel cocktail lounge. "Get some clothes on," he said.

"Why? The two of you have seen everything there is to see," she answered.

"Because I say so," Benjamin said. "And do it now."

"What the fuck do you guys want?" Eddie finally asked.

"You got something on?" Benjamin called out,

just as the woman came out of the bedroom wrapped in a large bath towel.

"There was nothing else," she told him.

"Okay, in the kitchen, Eddie, and Miss—"

"Name's Doris," the woman said.

Benjamin had Eddie and Doris sit at the table, while he and Markham stood; then to Eddie, he said, "Your friend Lucky is a very interesting man, more interesting than you let on during our first chat."

Eddie looked around. "I need a cigarette," he said.

Benjamin shook his head. "What I need is a lot more important than what you need. I need answers, Eddie, to questions about Lucky."

"I already told you, he's a pimp."

"And you're in on the action, right?"

Eddie started to shake his head, but Markham grabbed him by his chin. "This is heavy stuff, shithead," he growled, "and you're caught between a rock and very hard place." Then he let go.

Eddie rubbed his jaw.

"You got a warrant to come in here?" Doris asked.

Benjamin pointed a finger at her, then at Eddie. "Tell her if we need a warrant. Go on and tell her."

"Don't mix in this, Doris," Eddie said.

"I was only trying to help," she answered, pushing back her mousy brown hair. She was a short skinny woman, with a flat face and mousy brown hair. Her sad eyes matched the color of her hair. Even her breasts, from the small bulge they made under the towel, didn't have much to them.

"Lucky," Benjamin said, unwrapping the cellophane from a cigar, "tell me about you and Lucky."

"Alright, I had something going with him," Eddie said. "Okay, you guys satisfied now." His eyes went from them to Doris. "It was strictly business. I never touched any of his broads."

"You bastard!" she flung at him. "You fucking bastard. Was that your game?"

"Listen, Doris, the two of you can settle this problem later," Markham said. "Now it's lover boy's turn to sing us a sweet song." And grabbing Eddie by his jaw again, he wrenched his head around.

Eddie howled in pain. "You're going to rip my fucking jaw off!"

"Just might," Markham answered calmly.

Benjamin had already lit and was smoking his cigar before he said, "Tell me about Lucky's bigshot lawyer friend."

Eddie squirmed. "Lucky had a lot of clout. He had connections all over."

"Especially in D.C., right, Eddie?" Markham asked.

"You already know, so why are you asking me," Eddie said.

Markham knocked Eddie off the chair.

"Is he some kind of fucking nut?" Eddie almost screamed.

"The three guys that were wasted in the motel, Eddie, were taking turns with his girlfriend," Benjamin said. "He's fucking crazy now!"

Fear spilled into Eddie's face.

"Get back on the chair," Markham ordered.

Eddie hesitated.

"Better do what he tells you," Benjamin said,

blowing smoke down at Eddie. "Good. It's more comfortable on the chair than on the floor, isn't it?"

"It ain't comfortable—"

"Ever hear the name Lotz?" Markham asked.

"Yeah, he's one of Lucky's bigshot lawyer contacts. He does work for some of the embassies too. Lucky know guys in the Libyan Embassy."

"He told you that?" Benjamin asked.

"He's not much of a drinker and one afternoon he got tight after a couple of brews."

"Now comes the big question, Eddie," Benjamin said. "Listen real carefully, because on this one, if you don't give us the right answer—well, we can go a couple of ways . . . and I guarantee you won't like any of them. Now here it comes, Eddie. The only guys you sent to Lucky were Navy officers, isn't that right, Eddie, and that's because they were the only guys Lucky wanted to do business with—isn't that right, Eddie?"

After a few moments of silence, Eddie mumbled, "Mostly."

Benjamin took a deep drag on the cigar and slowly blew a column of smoke up toward the ceiling. "And who were the others, those who weren't Navy officers."

"Older guys—guys like yourself, looking for young stuff."

"Disgusting!" Doris screamed, suddenly launching herself at Eddie and beating him with her fists.

Markham grabbed ahold of Doris's bare shoulder and pushed her back in the chair.

The towel covering her opened and dropped to

the floor.

"Bitch," Eddie shouted, trying to wipe away the blood coming out of his nose. "Bitch."

"Cover yourself," Benjamin said.

Crying, Doris picked up the towel and wrapped it around herself again. "I feel like shit, just like shit, Eddie. I was beginning to think that we had something—"

He waved her silent. "You wanted to fuck so we fucked," he told her. "Nothing else!"

Doris put her arms down on the table and, sobbing, she buried her face in them.

"Okay, Eddie, get dressed and we'll take a ride down to Headquarters," Benjamin said.

"But I told you everything you wanted to know," Eddie whined.

"Yeah, that's why you're going down to Headquarters," Markham said. "We want to make sure that you don't get a chance to become involved with anyone like Lucky for a long, long time."

"You don't have anything on me," Eddie said.

"Doris?" Benjamin called.

She lifted her head, looked at Eddie and, still sobbing, she said, "I heard what he said and I'll tell the court."

"Get dressed, shithead," Markham snapped.

Hacker was seated in front of the sonar display and Howard was at the diving controls.

Forbushe, Tull and Smith were almost in the center of the control room. Neither one of them

228

spoke, since Forbushe had pointed a .357 at him and told him he'd blow his brains out if he did anything in the least bit suspicious—and that had happened two hours before. During the two hours, each of them had silently made his own inspection of the instruments that monitored the boat's various systems.

"We're being read," Hacker said, suddenly breaking the silence.

Forbushe rushed to him. "What—"

"Probably a chopper," he said, pointing to a small black box next to the sonar display scope. "The flashing red light means that someone topside is checking the magnetic variations."

"Flank speed," Forbushe shouted. "Helmsman, full right rudder."

"Flank speed, answered," Tull responded, putting down the phone.

"Full right rudder," the helmsman repeated.

The red flashing lessened and then went out altogether.

"Lost us," Hacker said.

Forbushe moved back to the center of the control room. "It had to be an American chopper. The Russians don't have any of their carriers in this area."

"Is that a question or a statement?" Smith asked.

Forbushe glared at him, but didn't answer.

"They don't have any carriers in this area," Tull said, and then to further disturb Forbushe, he added, "I'm not convinced that we received an authentic message, and if we didn't, our friends

229

might be out searching for us."

"The message was absolutely authentic," Forbushe said. "I explained why you weren't previously told about it."

Tull didn't answer. Forbushe was already upset about the possibility of carriers being in the area.

"They're ours," Smith said. "That chopper had to come from one of ours."

"Shut the fuck up," Forbushe shouted, pushing his face close to Smith's. "I don't want to hear you, understand. You keep your mouth shut until I ask you a question."

Moving close to them, Tull said, "Come on, Bill, ease up. We knew it wouldn't be easy when we started and it's probably going to get a lot tougher before it's over. The skipper is probably right. That chopper is probably off one of the two carriers in the Med."

Forbushe stepped back and, turning away from Smith, took a deep breath and exhaled before he said, "Out here from the Med?"

Tull nodded. "By now—well, who knows what has been figured out by now?"

"They couldn't have figured it out so fast and deployed—"

"Sure they could," Tull answered with a shrug. "Especially if there was a fluke—something we hadn't counted on happening, happened."

Forbushe ran his hand over his face. "Send someone down to the galley for coffee," he said.

"I could use a cup myself," Tull responded and, turning to the man who had manned the diving controls before Hacker took over again, he said,

"Bring coffee up to the control room for everyone, and if there are any sandwiches left, bring those too." Then with a smile, he faced Forbushe. "One of the first things I'm going to do when we reach Tripoli is sit down to a good dinner. That is, of course, if we make it. What about you, Bill?"

Forbushe looked away.

21

Captain Maylee was on the bridge when *Blue King Four* reported a contact, gave the coordinates and, in a matter of minutes, lost it. "*Blue King Four*, this is Blue Base, continue to search," Maylee ordered over the radio.

"Aye, aye, Skipper," the chopper pilot answered, recognizing the skipper's nasal twang.

Maylee left the captain's chair and walked to the starboard side of the bridge. He was a tall, lean man with a sharp nose and thin lips. He had been a fighter pilot during the Vietnam War and in three tours of duty managed to knock down a total of eight MIGS and escape from the Viet Cong after having been shot down over south Vietnam by a hand-held surface-to-air missile launcher on a strafing run. Finding the *C-1* and either forcing it to surrender or destroying it, would guarantee him his two stars. He stopped and looked out over the ocean. Finding a submarine, especially with the operating capabilities of the *C-1*, was like trying to find the proverbial needle in the haystack. Then, even as he was looking out at the sea, he suddenly became aware the clouds were moving in and that the color of the sea and the sky was changing. He turned around and was just about to ask for a meteorological update, when the OOD said, "Skipper, Met reports a tropical storm is moving in from the southeast and moving west. Met advises to expect heavy rains and winds gusting to thirty knots or more."

"Order *Blue King Four* to return immediately," Maylee said.

"Aye, aye, Skipper," the OOD answered.

Maylee resumed his place in the captain's chair. A severe deterioration in the weather would make him depend completely on this escort vessel to locate the *C-1*. He pursed his lips. The damn storm might just give the *C-1* the chance to slip into the Med.

After two hours, Forbushe ordered the *C-1* back on its original course. "Whoever was reading us is well out of range by now, and I want to bring this mission to an end as soon as possible."

"That's for sure," Tull answered. Forbushe was holding up better than he'd expected him to. Time was running out. Sooner or later the Russians or the Americans would find them and all hell would break loose. He needed to think things out without the distraction of Forbushe being present. Moving close to Smith, he whispered, "Keep your mouth shut and don't do anything you won't be able to undo. The man is tightly wound."

Smith looked at him questioningly.

"What the hell are you two whispering about?" Forbushe demanded to know.

"I was telling him not to bug," Tull answered before Smith could.

"Why, where the hell are you going?"

"I need about a half-hour sacktime," Tull said. "I've got a roaring headache that won't quit." And even as he spoke, he found himself looking at a way to take control of the boat—that, he suddenly realized was his only hope of either stopping Forbushe from getting the *C-1* to Tripoli or preventing the *C-1* from being sunk by whoever could get to her first. Whether it would be the Russians or the Americans made no difference to him—until he and the *C-1* were safe, both were enemies.

"I could use some myself," Forbushe admitted.

Tull made no comment and walked out of the control room to his cabin. His muscles ached, as much from the tension of the situation as from the long hours in the control room. He stretched out in his bunk with his hands behind his head and began to revolve in his mind the idea of taking control of the *C-1* in much the same manner that a diamond cutter might examine a raw diamond to discover the best way to cleave it. The boat had to be driven to the surface, and the quickest way to do that was to start a fire. It was also the most dangerous. It might quickly get out of control, or it might send Forbushe out of control . . .

Tull's eyelids became heavy and he had to force himself to keep them open. Anything involving the

235

boat's operating systems would immediately alert Forbushe. No, the action had to be direct and have absolute consequences. That way Forbushe wouldn't have the slightest doubt—"

The 1MC came on. "Tull to the control room, on the double . . . Tull to the control room."

Tull bolted out of a doze. That was unmistakably Forbushe. He sat up and swung his feet down on the deck.

The 1MC blared his name again.

Leaving his cabin, Tull mumbled, "Now what the fuck do you want?" As soon as he reached the bridge, the tableau was clear. Forbushe was holding Hacker and Smith at gunpoint and Howard was down on the deck, crumpled into a fetal position. He was bleeding profusely from the stomach.

Tull bent over him. Blood was beginning to trickle out of the side of Howard's mouth. He felt for the neck pulse. It was very weak. He looked up at Forbushe and shook his head; then he asked, "What happened?"

"I caught him trying to sabotage the diving controls," Forbushe said.

"How?" Tull asked.

"Blow all ballast."

Tull looked down at Howard. Now there was one less man he could depend on.

"I want these two put down again," Forbushe said. "We can make it to Tripoli without them."

"We'll never do it, Bill. Never."

"We—"

The pitched ping of a sonar filled the *C-1*.

"Get to the sonar," Tull ordered Hacker.

Forbushe was too stunned to move.

"Flank speed," Tull yelled.

"Flank speed answered," Smith said, holding the engine-room phone.

"Stand by at the dive controls," Tull said.

"Standing by at the diving controls," the man who'd operated them before answered.

"Take her up five hundred quickly," Tull ordered.

"Up five hundred," the man responded. "Diving planes ten up."

Tull's eyes went to the depth gauge.

The pinging faded.

"Do you get a fix?" Tull asked, still watching the depth gauge rewind.

"Negative. But I ran their sound through the computer. Distant and weak . . . but I got an Alpha."

"You sure?"

"As sure as the computer is. It says Alpha, so I'm telling you Alpha."

"One thousand feet," the man at the dive controls said.

"The C-1 went up another fifty, then settled down at one thousand.

"Trimmed to the mark," the diving-control operator said. "Diving planes at zero."

Using the back of his arm, Tull wiped the sweat from his brow. "We need Hacker and the skipper," he said, "and if I were you, I would consider bringing the diving control and at least one man to relieve Hacker and the DCO."

237

"Get them," Forbushe said, snapping the safety in place on the .357 and putting it in his belt.

In Washington, the morning grew into the afternoon and the President canceled all of his appointments to work on the speech to the nation. In the past, his speeches, though often written by him, were polished and sometimes, because of his sense of humor, sanitized, as he called it, by a team of professional speech writers. Having a sense of humor over national television was unbecoming the leader of the most powerful nation in the world and, according to his advisers, it gave a great deal of ammunition to his opposition, something no politician should ever consciously do.

But by the middle of the afternoon, the President hadn't completed a single page, and rereading the page he had written, he crumpled it up and threw it into the wastepaper basket; then he stood up, turned around and faced the window that looked out on the rose garden. The President was no stranger to war. He'd been a naval officer in "the brown water navy," as was called the boats and men who fought in the Mekong River Delta and later up north, near the border with north Vietnam. As a lieutenant, he'd commanded a squadron and knew all too well what it felt like to be shot at and how it felt to kill another human being. It had been sometime during his tour of duty that he'd made up his mind that if he survived 'Nam, he'd dedicate himself to peace, and though politics could hardly be termed "peaceful," it offered him the way to pursue his goal. And now, after coming to a place, during his administration, where the United States and the Russians not only limited arms production across the board, but also shared scientific and technical data, the two nations were once again on a collision course and—

The phone on his desk rang.

Annoyed that his trend of thought had been interrupted, when he had given explicit instructions that he didn't want to take any phone calls, he pursed his lips and turned around.

A green signal light flashed, indicating that the Russian premier was on the Moscow hotline.

The President picked up the phone. Early in his relationship with the premier, he discovered that the man spoke perfect English and he had set to and succeeded in gaining some mastery in Russian.

"Mister President," the Russian premier said, "I have something to tell you which I am sure will help you evaluate the current crisis in its true perspective."

"I'm listening, Mister Premier," the President answered. "The present situation is far from what we have had between our two countries during my term in office."

"There was a man, a KGB officer named Serge Petrov, who had been in your country for several years."

"He is dead," the President said.

"Yes, we know that, but we also know he had been involved in various activities on behalf of another nation."

"Do you mean the activities that have led our two nations to their present predicament?"

"We too," the premier said, "would not be overjoyed to see your submarine in the wrong hands."

"Am I to understand that your people—that is to say that the KGB or any other group under your jurisdiction was not involved in the killing of our men and hijacking of our submarine."

"Absolutely not," the premier said. "I have waited this long to inform you, only because I did not have all the facts."

"Can you reveal what nation, or nations, is responsible?"

"It is one with whom you have had difficulty in the past," the premier answered and then he said, "I will withdraw my missile-carrying submarines from their positions along your coasts if you do the same and withdraw your ships from the North Atlantic approaches to the Arctic."

"Consider it done," the President answered with a sigh of relief.

"I will do one more thing to show you our good faith. I offer you the use of three attack submarines that are presently in the South Atlantic, some four hundred miles east of the Strait of Gibraltar, which puts them within two hundred miles of your carrier battle group."

"And, Mister Premier," the President responded, "what would we do without our spies in the sky?"

The premier laughed. "We would, I am sure, find other ways to watch one another."

"Do you think there will ever come a time when neither of our countries will feel that it is necessary to do that?" the President asked.

"Truthfully, Mister President, I do not see that happening for a long time. But you and me—well, even with the spies in the skies, we have found trust."

"We certainly have," the President said. "And I will accept the use of those three attack submarines. But their captains must not, I repeat, they must not use any force. They will search for the submarine, and if they find it, they must report its position to the captain of the *America*, whose battle group is closest to the area where the submarine was last located. Do the captains of those submarines speak English?"

"Certainly, Mister President. They would not be allowed to command a row boat, let alone an attack submarine, if they were not fluent in English, as well as German. Does your captain speak Russian."

"I do not know, but my guess is that he does not," the President answered.

"There is one more item, Mister President," the premier said.

"Yes," the President responded, wondering if this was going to be the proverbial kicker.

"My people are sure you have a mole—a person close to you."

For a moment, the President was stunned, but then he realized that the premier was referring to Tull and Forbushe. And regaining his composure, he responded, "I will certainly consider what you just said very carefully."

"Your operational orders, Mister President, will

241

immediately be transmitted to the captains of the three submarines."

"Thank you for calling, Mister Premier," the President said.

"It was a good conversation," the premier answered.

The line went dead.

The President put the phone down, smiled and began to whistle, then off-key he sang, "Oh What a Beautiful Day." Then, picking up the phone, he punched out the numbers that would connect him to the CNO. "Except for the Sixth Fleet, I am canceling the full alert. I want all ships and aircraft to return to their normal operating status."

"Mister President—"

"I have just been assured by the Russian premier that none of their people were involved in the hijacking of *Command One*," the President said.

"But a KGB agent was involved with Commanders Tull and Forbushe," Admiral Fletcher countered.

The President was about to reveal that Petrov was a double agent and that he'd operated under instructions from a government other than the Russian, but he stopped himself and instead he repeated his instructions, adding, to make sure the admiral understood, "I am not suggesting that these things be done. I am, in my constitutional role of Commander in Chief, ordering that they be done."

"Yes, Mister President," the CNO responded.

"And there is one more thing," the President said, and he explained that three Russian attack submarines would be cooperating with the *America*'s carrier battle group.

"I will immediately transmit this information to Captain Maylee," the CNO replied.

The President could tell from the sound of Fletcher's voice that he wasn't in the least bit happy, especially with the idea of having Russian submarines working so close to the *America*'s battle group and he told him, "Admiral, cooperation beats shooting anytime." Without waiting for Fletcher to answer, he hung up and in the same off-key voice, he continued to sing "Oh What a Beautiful Day."

22

Forbushe, with a coffee mug in his hand and leaning against the starboard bulkhead in the control room, was fully aware that there were only five crew members involved in the operation of the control room, but, if he could count on Tull, and that, his intuition told him, was a big *if,* he had double their number. The rest of the crew was still down and would have to be kept down until they reached Tripoli. But what Tull didn't know—and he was sure that Harry hadn't told him—was that the longer the men were kept under the influence of the toxin, the more probability that some would not be able to be brought back and would suffer some sort of permanent nerve damage. Even as these thoughts moved through his mind, Forbushe's eyes drifted over to Hacker and Peter Ho, a nineteen-year-old Chinese American, whose ears were even better attuned to the undersea sounds than Hacker's. Suddenly, he realized they had something and, before he could ask, Hacker said, "Multiple targets.

Bearing, two seven fiver. Range—"

"What the hell is the range?" Forbushe demanded, crowding Hacker at the sonar display.

"Range, off the scope," Hacker said in the same steady voice he'd use in a normal situation.

Forbushe glared at him. "What the fuck do you mean it's off the scope?"

"It's out of range," Hacker answered stiffly.

"I saw that blip . . . I saw it," Forbushe shouted. "You did something to the equipment." He dropped the mug of coffee and, yanking the .357 out of his belt, he pushed the muzzle under Hacker's chin. "Put the blip back on the display scope," he growled, "or you're dead."

Everyone in the control room froze.

"It can't be done."

"You mean you won't do it," Forbushe screamed.

"Multiple targets," Ho quietly announced. "Bearing, two seven five . . . Range, twenty-five thousand yards . . . Speed, thirty knots . . . Depth, eight hundred even . . . Course, eight five, closing."

Forbushe still had the muzzle pushed hard against Hacker's chin. He looked at the display scope. The three targets were plainly visible; then, almost as an afterthought, he lowered the weapon, put the safety back on and returned it to inside his belt.

"Two Alphas and a Zulu," Ho said, reading the data on the computer.

Tull moved up to the sonar station; then, turning to Smith, he said, "They can do a good job of boxing us in. We better find a thermocline, or go deep and run silent for a while."

"We can outrun them," Forbushe said.

"Probably. But we might run ourselves into friends of theirs," Tull answered.

Forbushe clenched his hand into a fist and for several moments he gnawed on his knuckles. He couldn't afford to take time to either find a safe spot in a thermocline or go deep and run silent, which meant running very slow. "Go to flank speed," he said. "We'll outrun them."

Tull nodded at Smith.

"Flank speed," Smith said.

"Flank speed answered," the man at the telephone responded.

Forbushe moved back to the bulkhead and leaned against it. He wished he could close his eyes.

Captain Maylee read the radio message just handed him by the OOD. "I don't fucking believe it!" he exploded. "The next damn thing we'll be told is—" He stopped, realizing that every member of the bridge watch was looking at him and smiling. His explosion into obscenities was characteristic and gave the crew something to laugh about. He smiled sheepishly and, talking to everyone on the bridge, he said, "None of you even heard what I just said."

"Yes, sir," the OOD answered for everyone. "We didn't."

"Have the communications officer alert his men for incoming messages from Soviet submarines," he said. "As soon as one of them makes contact, patch the transmission to the bridge."

"Aye, aye, sir," the OOD responded.

Maylee looked out toward the bow end of the

flight deck. "Met says we're in for at least another two to three hours of rain and wind. Their best guess is that this storm is going to become a full-fledged hurricane by the time it gets halfway across the Atlantic."

The OOD didn't answer.

"Better notify our escorts that their sonar men are liable to pick up a couple of Alphas and a Zulu. If that happens, I want to be informed immediately."

"Yes, sir."

Frowning, Maylee commented, "The Ruskie sub drivers can speak English, can you beat that?" Then, shaking his head, he added, "And I can't speak or understand any goddamn thing more than *da* and *nyet.*"

After Benjamin and Markham visited Admiral Corliss and told him about Forbushe's connection to Lucky, the pimp, who turned out to be a Libyan national with very high Washington connections, including the lawyer, Lotz, who did work for several embassies including the Libyan, the admiral provided them with a chopper to take them to Washington and also arranged to have a limo and a driver meet them at the National Airport. But just before Benjamin and Markham left the admiral's office, Benjamin said, "I don't think you should call anyone in Washington and tell them what I've just told you, or that Guy and I are going up there to pay Lotz a visit."

"I'm sure the President would want to know, especially about the Libyan—"

"Admiral, I've done a lot of thinking about what has been going down," Benjamin said as he relit a cigar that had gone out, "and as the expression goes, 'Something is rotten in Denmark,' only it's not in Denmark that something is rotten, but in Washington."

Corliss squinted at him. "I'm not sure I get your drift."

"There's got to be a leak . . . Don't look so surprised."

"Captain Pilcher—"

"He was one, but he's history and he had to report to someone else, and that someone has to be in Washington."

"Are you sure?"

Benjamin rolled the cigar from the left side of his mouth to the right. "Admiral, if I didn't have to trust you, I wouldn't."

Corliss's jaw dropped.

"Does that tell you how sure I am?" Benjamin said.

"You certainly made your point, Detective Benjamin."

"In my business you learn to do that after you get shot, firebombed and waste a couple of guys in the act of raping your partner's girlfriend. When those kinds of things happen, you get to feel kind of crowded and not by circumstances."

Corliss stepped out from behind his desk to walk Benjamin and Markham to the door. "You'll call and let me know what you found," he said.

"We'll let you know, Admiral," Benjamin answered and, as he followed Markham out of the door, Markham stopped and asked, "Admiral, who authorized Tull and Forbushe's transfer to the *C-1*?"

"We arranged Tull's. Why?"

"Are you sure that no one else was involved in his transfer?"

"I don't know. It took a lot of doing to get BuPers to make the transfer."

"What about Forbushe?"

The admiral shook his head.

"When was Pilcher assigned to your office?" Benjamin asked.

"A year ago, give or take a couple of months."

"Could you check BuPers?" Markham asked.

"What would I be looking for?"

Benjamin said, "Anything that might seem irregular—a change of procedure from the normal mechanics involved in the transfer of a man from one assignment to another."

"You think—"

Benjamin smiled. "It takes some doing to put the right men in the right place at the right time when they have a very specific assignment to carry out. And these men certainly had that kind of specific assignment."

"Then there is no longer any need for you to go on the air this evening," Hubbered said, standing in front of the President's desk.

"Sit down, Brett," the President said. "You look kind of at sixes and sevens with yourself."

Hubbered sat down. "These past few days have been hectic. I'm not sure that I totally understand

250

the reason for your canceling the full alert."

The President bounced forward in his chair, planted his elbows on the desk and said, "The problem was never the Soviets."

"But Petrov was a known KGB agent and was connected to Tull and Forbushe."

The President shook his head. "He was a double agent. He worked for— Brett are you feeling well?"

"I have the feeling I'm coming down with a summer cold," Hubbered answered.

"I'll call my physician now," the President said, reaching for the phone.

"No need to," Hubbered said. "I think I need sleep more than anything else. If you can spare me the rest of the afternoon, I'd like to go home and sleep."

"Go with my blessings," the President responded. "Have one of your people notify the TV and radio networks that I will not be speaking tonight." He leaned back. "You can't imagine how wonderful I feel at this moment."

"I certainly share your feelings, Mister President," Hubbered said and began retreating toward the door.

"Take good care of yourself, Brett," the President told him.

"I intend to do just that," Hubbered answered.

Lotz's office was in the Watergate Hotel. He had a river view, a beautiful dark-haired secretary, deep pile wall-to-wall brown carpeting and a winning smile.

"What can I do for you gentlemen?" he asked,

shaking each of their hands before suggesting they be more informal and occupy the deep club chairs set around a glass-topped coffee table.

"I'm the detective who arrested your friend Lucky," Benjamin said, smiling at Lotz.

"And you're the man who sprung him," Markham added.

Lotz froze; then a twisted smile formed on his lips. "I hope neither of you have a problem with that," he said. "It was all done perfectly legally."

"Never a doubt about that in either of our minds," Benjamin said.

"Then I don't understand the reason for your visit," Lotz responded, looking at Benjamin, then at Markham and finally back at Benjamin.

Markham suddenly stood up and walked to the window. "Imagine," he said, "twenty floors down to the river." Then he went to the door and locked it.

"Just what do you think you're doing?" Lotz questioned, starting to stand.

But Benjamin was up first and rammed his fist into Lotz's stomach.

The man doubled up and dropped back into the chair. "You're finished," Lotz gasped, his face contorted with pain and tears coming out of his eyes. "The two of you—"

Benjamin backhanded him.

Blood suddenly streaked Lotz's chin.

"Okay," Markham said, "now you know where we're coming from and we know where you're coming from."

Lotz shook his head.

Benjamin grabbed Lotz's necktie, rolled it around

his hand and jerked it hard, forcing Lotz's head down. "Tell us about your Libyan connection."

"My neck—"

"I'll break your fucking neck," Benjamin growled, "if you don't tell me everything you know about Libya's role in the hijacking of the *C-1*."

"Bring him to the window," Markham said. "We'll throw the son of a bitch out of it!"

Suddenly a stain spread over the front of Lotz's trousers.

"He's pissed in his pants!" Markham exclaimed derisively.

"The two of you could be millionaires," Lotz said.

"He doesn't understand," Benjamin commented. "He just doesn't understand that he's in deep shit, and that he's in no position to make any offers, because he doesn't have anything to offer."

Lotz screwed his eyes up. "Lucky kept tabs on Forbushe."

"A good opener," Markham said. "Tell us more."

"Forbushe works for the Libyan government."

"You mean he's a spy?"

"A spy like you," Benjamin said.

"And Tull?" Markham added.

"Yes," Lotz said with a loud exhalation.

"Who recruited them?"

"Forbushe came to us. He believes in the Arab cause. Despite his English-sounding name. He is an Arab. His father and mother were Arabs."

"What about Tull?"

Lotz shook his head. "I had nothing to do with him. He was run by someone else."

Markham grabbed his hair and started to pull it

back when the phone rang. "Saved by the bell," he commented.

There was a phone on the top of the coffee table with a speaker and voice amplifier.

"Answer it," Benjamin said.

"It's Mister Hubbered," Lotz's secretary said. "He wants you to meet him at his home as soon as possible. He says it's urgent."

Lotz thanked her and switched off.

Benjamin grinned broadly. "You certainly do know some very important people in this town, don't you." Then he said, "I'm sure you have a change of clothes here. Guy here will keep an eye on you while you put on something less telling; then the three of us will pay a visit to our friend Mister Hubbered."

"Cm'on, let's get you changed," Markham told Lotz as he reached down and lifted him to his feet.

"We'll take the beautiful woman out there at the front desk with us," Markham said.

"She doesn't know anything about this," Lotz protested on the way to the bathroom.

"Maybe, maybe not," Benjamin answered. "But just to be sure that she doesn't make any calls to your Libyan friends, she'll go with us."

23

Hubbered paced the length of the study in his Tudor-designed house, located at the end of a tree-lined cul-de-sac. Two bearded men were with him. One leaned against the wall and, smoking a cigarette, sometimes blew smoke rings. The other, Rashied, who was the heavier of the two, sat in the rocking chair by the stone hearth, looking at a set of bare wrought-iron andirons.

"They're coming here," Hubbered said, stopping to look at the man blowing smoke rings. "And they're bringing her with them."

"We'll be waiting," Rashied answered.

"You don't understand, Karium, that—"

"We will take care of the situation," Rashied said, rocking back and forth. "You have nothing to concern yourself about."

Hubbered started to pace again. "It's only a matter of time before the whole scheme becomes unraveled."

"Time is what we are playing for," Karium

answered. "Time. With enough time the submarine will be in Tripoli."

Hubbered stopped again.

"There's a small plane waiting for us at an airport not far from here," Rashied said, rocking slowly back and forth.

"She comes with us," Hubbered said. His eyes flew to Karium.

"If you wish," Karium said with a knowing smile. "Ah, love, what would we do without it?"

"How will we get out of here?" Hubbered questioned.

"We have something they want. Like you, my dear Mister Hubbered, the two detectives are emotionally involved with women."

"You have them here?"

The two men laughed.

"Certainly they are here," Karium answered.

Rashied stood up. "We'll be close by," he said, motioning to Karium. "In the meantime, until they show up, try to relax. After all, you want to be able to take care of your lady friend when the time comes and you won't be able to even get your cock up, much less use it, if you work yourself into a heart attack."

The two of them laughed and left the study.

Hubbered went to the window and stationed himself there. From it, he could see the roadway leading to the house.

"Mister President, this is Admiral Corliss," he said, identifying himself because he was using a special scrambler phone.

"If you're calling about my cancellation of the full alert, I—"

"Excuse me, sir, but I am not calling about that," Corliss said. "I have something entirely different to discuss with you."

"Please, tell me what it is."

Corliss hesitated; then, clearing his throat, he said, "I had reason to check—"

The President wasn't sure how to react to Corliss's inability to say what he had to say. He knew the man well enough to know that Corliss regretted his role and, after a suitable period of time had passed, he would probably resign of his own accord, coming up with a suitable explanation to save face.

"Mister President, there have been several irregularities at BuPers under your direction."

"Just what the hell are you talking about?" the President shouted. Springing to his feet and still holding the phone, he walked to the back of the chair.

"Requests from you to transfer Commanders Tull and Forbushe to the *C-1*," Corliss said.

"What? I never made those requests, and until I heard their names I never knew that either Tull or Forbushe existed."

"Mister Hubbered—"

"Hubbered?" the President questioned.

"The notes came from him, but in both cases the substance was that he was writing on your behalf and that you'd be most appreciative if both these officers were transferred to the *C-1*, and prior to that he requested that Captain Pilcher be assigned to my

257

staff, as my personal aide."

"You can, of course, prove everything you just told me?" the President asked.

"Yes, Mister President. Tull was one of ours, yes. But Mister Hubbered could not have known that, when he requested the transfer. That transfer had been requested for an entirely different reason; namely, to have Tull take part in the hijacking of *C-1*."

"Absolutely unbelievable—Hubbered is the mole." The President sat down.

"I'm sorry," Corliss said. "I know how close he was to you."

"I'll take care of it," the President said. "And I would appreciate your silence on the matter, at least for the present."

"You have my word, Mister President," Corliss answered.

The President put the scrambler phone down, sat back in his chair and closed his eyes. Brett Hubbered was a friend, a trusted adviser, the man to whom he'd confided his fears, doubts and hopes. He had known him practically all of his life. Brett was an usher at his wedding and would have been the best man, if—

The President opened his eyes and spun around in his swivel chair. "I never knew you, Brett," he whispered sadly, "and I thought I did." He stood up and walked to the window. He had known disappointment and despair before. His favorite brother had been shot down in a dog fight with an MIG over Korea. A younger sister was in an institution for the retarded and another brother, an up-and-coming senator, had been shot and killed by a sociopath. But the unhappiness resulting from those traumas were caused by circumstances beyond his control. Brett was a different story. He had chosen him. No, that was not quite right either. They had chosen each other. As far back as their university days, when he had harbored aspirations of becoming a novelist, Brett had understood that he was more of a political animal than he had realized. He remembered Brett saying, "Go for the brass ring and I'll help you get it. I'll be the king maker and you be the king."

The President pursed his lips. "It really worked that way, Brett," he said. "It really happened." Then he turned and looked at the phone. There wasn't any other way. He left the window, sat down at the desk again and, picking up the phone, he punched out the direct number to the Director of the FBI, Harold Otis.

"Otis here," the clipped voice said.

"This is the President. You are directed to arrest Mister Brett Hubbered and impound the contents of his office and home."

A silence followed, punctuated only by the sound of Otis's breathing.

Finally Otis asked, "On what charge, Mister President?"

"Treason," the President answered in a whisper.

"I'm sorry, Mister President, I didn't hear what you said."

"I said, treason," he snapped.

Again there were several moments of silence, but this time it was broken by the President. "I want this carried out expeditiously. I don't want the media to get even a sniff of this until—"

"Excuse me, Mister President, how do we handle the situation if Mister Hubbered offers resistance?"

The President ran his free hand over his eyes. He hadn't thought about that possibility, or if he had, he had put it out of his mind so quickly that it seemed as if it had never entered at all.

"It might go that way," Otis said.

"Damn it, I know it could!" the President exploded.

A third silence settled heavily between them and again it was the President who brought it to an end by saying, "I've never known Brett to be a violent man, but you must protect your people, I fully understand and approve of that. Use whatever force you must to subdue and arrest Mister Hubbered. I want you to take charge of the operation personally."

"Yes, Mister President," Otis answered.

"Thank you, Harold," the President said and, putting the phone down, he placed his hands behind his head, turned toward the rose garden and felt a growing tightness in his throat. "This isn't supposed to be the way the script goes," he said, forcing the words out and at the same time, shaking his head.

"Those were Russian subs," Smith said to Tull as the two of them drank coffee in the wardroom. "And they're not just out there for fun and games."

"We can outrun them," Tull answered, "and probably with our equipment outmaneuver them until—"

Suddenly there was shouting—some of it English, but the rest of it in Arabic.

Tull and Smith ran toward the control room, but before they reached it two shots exploded; then three more.

"What the hell is happening?" Tull roared, entering the control room first. The space was filled with the acrid stink of burnt gunpowder. He didn't see Forbushe. But Hacker and Bright were armed and the sonar operator's right arm was full of blood. "Those fucking shots are going to pinpoint us."

"Tull, it's over for you and your men," Forbushe shouted from the passageway toward the bow. "Tell Hacker and Bright to drop their guns and throw them out here."

Tull glared at Hacker and Bright. "What happened?"

"We decided to make our play," Hacker said.

Tull looked at Smith. "You know about this 'play?'" And before Smith could answer, he said, "Yeah, just from the look on your face, I know you knew about it. It was some fucking play."

"I'll kill a member of the crew every ten minutes unless you surrender now," Forbushe shouted.

"How many rounds do each of you have?" Tull asked.

They checked their magazines of their snub nose .38's.

"Four," Hacker said.

"Three," Bright answered.

"We have the arms locker," Forbushe yelled.

Tull knew the longer he could delay answering, the angrier Forbushe would become.

"Don't risk it, Tull," Forbushe shouted.

"If they rush us, we're dead," Smith said.

"If we surrender, we might as well be dead," Tull responded. He looked toward the wounded man. "One of you fucking players put a tourniquet on that man's arm or he'll bleed to death." Then he decided to challenge Forbushe. "I'm taking her to the surface," Tull said in as calm a voice as he could muster.

Instantly Forbushe shouted, "They'll find us!"

Tull took the .38 from Hacker and said to Bright, "Give yours to Haines. He's going to send a couple of guys through that bulkhead opening. Be ready for them." The last thing he wanted was a shootout a thousand feet below the ocean's surface.

"Tull—"

"All hands, stand by to surface," Tull said over the 1MC.

An instant later, a sustained burst from an M-16, and a man rushed toward the control room.

Tull and Haines fired simultaneously.

The man kept coming; suddenly he faltered and threw out his arms, as if he pushed violently against something. The next instant he crashed down on the deck, the top half of his body inside the control room.

Tull dropped to the deck, bellied over to the body, pulled the M-16 out of the dead man's hands and the extra magazine from his belt. Scrambling to his feet some distance from the open bulkhead door, he shouted, "Surface. Take her up!"

Suddenly the ping of a sonar probe sounded throughout the boat.

"Hard right rudder," Smith ordered. "Stand by on diving controls."

"Hard right rudder," the helmsman responded.

"Down five hundred feet," Smith ordered.

Bright repeated the order.

"Target bearing, nine five . . . Range, twenty thousand yards . . . Speed, forty knots . . . Depth, nine five zero . . . Closing . . . ID, Alpha class submarine."

"Tull, the shooting is over," Forbushe yelled. "We have to talk."

"Second target, bearing two—"

The pinging sound of several different sonar probes filled the *C-1*.

"Second target, bearing two five . . . Range, eighteen thousand yards. Depth, twelve hundred . . . Closing . . . ID, Alpha class submarine."

"I'm coming in," Forbushe said.

Tull didn't answer.

Captain Maylee was in his sea cabin. Though a five-foot sea was running and the sky was still overcast, the rain had stopped and the forecast was good enough to send out three Sea Kings to continue the search for the *C-1*.

Maylee was resting in his bunk. His eyes were closed and he was trying to decide whether to force himself to get up and go back to the bridge or let himself have the luxury of a short nap, when the decision was made for him by a knock at the door.

Maylee planted his feet on the deck and called out, "Come in."

A junior officer of the watch said, "Skipper, we have radio contact with a Zulu. The skipper requests to speak to you."

"Let's go!" Maylee said, already heading for the door. Within moments, he was in the radio room. "This is Captain Maylee," he announced, speaking into the mike handed to him by the communications officer.

"Captain, this is Captain Mikhail Gorin, I have sonar contact and I have ID'd the *Command One*. Her position is forty miles due east of your own position." And then he spelled it out in terms of latitude and longitude. "Two Alpha class submarines are tracking it; they will not move any closer than fifteen thousand yards. That should be sufficient distance for your destroyers to find and differentiate them from your target."

"I will repeat the position of the *C-1*," Maylee said and read it off the scrap of paper on which he'd jotted it down.

"Correct," Gorin answered.

"Thank you, Captain Gorin," Maylee responded.

"Good hunting, over and out," Gorin said.

Maylee put the mike down and, handing the communications officer the slip of paper, he said, "Get it out to the Sea Kings and our escorts. Under my orders send Knox out ahead of us." Then, picking up the phone to the CDC, Maylee ordered the launch of all the available Sea Kings.

The President's scrambler phone rang. "Yes,"

he answered.

"This is Captain Maylee. Captain Mikhail Goren has reported the position of *Command One*. I have taken the necessary steps to intercept it."

"Let me know when your people have located it," the President said. "I will be standing by."

"Yes, Mister President," Captain Maylee responded.

The President immediately put through a conference call to Admiral Hicks, commander of COMSUBLANT and Admiral Corliss and gave them the information that Maylee had given to him. Then he said, "Gentlemen, because of the rapidly developing situation, I want you here in Washington as soon as possible." He purposely did not make any specific reference to Hubbered and his instructions to the Director of the FBI.

Both then agreed to be in the capital within two hours.

The President put the phone down and, leaving the Oval Office, he went upstairs to the living quarters and found his wife, Charlotte, getting ready to take their two children, Andrew and Katherine, whom he called Kate, on a trip to the zoo.

"You look very tired," she said.

"I have a roaring headache," he told her and then he said, "Sit down, there's something I have to tell you."

She gave him a strange look.

He managed a smile. "I know I haven't shared much of my office with you."

"That's an understatement," she answered.

He took hold of her hands. "It makes very little

sense for two people to loose sleep over the same thing," he said.

"I might be able to ease the burden from time to time."

He shrugged. "You might just get that chance now. I've ordered the Director of the FBI to arrest Brett—"

"Oh my God!"

He nodded. "He is going to be charged with treason," he whispered.

"Brett?"

"For security reasons, I can't go into the details," he said. "But the facts—"

Suddenly she let go of his hands and, throwing her arms around him, she drew him to her and cradled his head against her breasts.

24

Tull and Forbushe confronted each other.

"There's fifteen million dollars waiting for you in Tripoli," Forbushe said. "Think of how you can live if you have that kind of money to spend."

"You never meant to deliver the *C-1* to primary negotiators," Tull said, still pretending to be the double agent.

"Come on, John," Forbushe responded, using his given name in an attempt to be friendly. "You knew what the situation was the moment I knew what the 'alternate destination' meant and you didn't. And if you didn't know by then, you must have figured it out by now."

Tull glanced over to Smith, then to Hacker and Bright. Their faces were full of tension. They were players in a game without knowing the rules, or even if the game had rules?

"That's why you were ordered to kill Harry," Forbushe said.

Nodding, Tull faced him. "I hadn't figured that

one out yet." The order to waste Harry had come from Hubbered.

Forbushe looked pleased. "It's refreshing to know that there are a few things that you hadn't figured out."

"I'm human too," Tull answered and, then smiling, he added, "Here's one *you* probably haven't figured out yet."

Instantly Forbushe's face lost its pleased expression.

"It's over, Forbushe," Tull said calmly. "You haven't figured that it never really began."

Forbushe cocked his head to one side.

Suddenly the printer attached to the ELF began to operate.

"How—" Forbushe started to say.

"Someone must have figured out we didn't go down," Tull answered, going to the printer, which was located in the communications room, a space within a few steps of the control room.

Forbushe started to follow.

"Stay where you are," Tull ordered.

Forbushe shook his head.

"Stay," Haines snapped, pointing his .38 at him.

Tull watched the letters print out. Between each there was a thirty-second time lapse, but as each word formed he read it aloud: "This is Captain Maylee, commander of Battle Group Ten . . . You have been located . . . You are ordered to immediately surface and surrender . . . You have two minutes to respond . . . At the end of that time we will take appropriate steps." Just as he stepped back into the control room, Forbushe yanked the 9mm out of his belt and began firing.

A round slammed into Tull's shoulder and dropped him to the desk.

Bright screamed.

Forbushe ran into the communications room and pumped three rounds into the radio gear. When he came out, Haines fired. Forbushe clutched his stomach, stumbled and went down on his knees.

Two men started to charge into the control room but Moussarakis squeezed off a short burst, killing them before they were two steps inside.

Still on his knees, Forbushe lifted his weapon and pointed it at Tull.

Moussarakis saw him and got off a burst.

The side of Forbushe's head opened and a fountain of blood spurted out. He fell to the deck, and for several moments his body twitched violently.

The sonar pinging started again, then it filled the *C-1*.

"Echo ranging," Hacker exclaimed. "They got us now."

Tull managed to pull himself to his feet. His left shoulder was bleeding and felt as if a hot poker had been rammed into it. He switched on the 1MC. "Mister Forbushe and two other men are dead. The two of you who still have weapons, move into the control room with your hands over your head now."

Suddenly an alarm went off and a red warning light began to flash on the fire indication board.

"Fire in the communications room," Smith said.

"Haines, Moussarakis, take care of it," Tull ordered as smoke was already beginning to drift into the control room.

Two men with their hands clasped behind their heads stepped through the bulkhead door.

Tull went over to Forbushe's body and, with his good hand, he pried the 9mm free from the dead man's hand. "Over there," Tull said to the two men, waving them to a corner.

"Ashcans on the way down," Hacker announced.

"Okay, Smith, it's up to you to get us the hell out of this," Tull said.

Two explosions within seconds of each other merged into one and smashed down on the *C-1*.

Tull lost his footing and went down. The 9mm fired.

One of the two men screamed and fell backward.

A coupling on an overhead pipe ruptured, sending a powerful column of water splashing into the control room.

"Get a wrench on that," Smith ordered.

Using his right hand, Tull cut the flow of water to a trickle.

"Got one fire out, but there's still stuff burning," Moussarakis shouted. "The smoke is very bad."

"Hard left rudder," Smith ordered.

"Hard left rudder," the helmsman answered.

"Take her down fast," Smith said.

"Diving plane down ten."

The *C-1*'s bow pitched downward.

"Flooding all tanks," Bright said.

"Four cans on the way down," Hacker said.

Tull picked himself up and watched the depth gauge's needle rapidly unwind.

The four ashcans exploded above and to the right of them. A shockwave shook them violently.

"Fifteen hundred feet," Bright announced.

"Two is the max," Tull responded, beginning to feel the effects of his wound and the smoke.

The pinging continued to fill the boat.

"Eighteen hundred feet," Hacker said. "There's bottom at twenty-one hundred."

Tull looked at the man, who still had his hands clasped behind his head. "You have a choice: you can help us get to the surface or you can die now." And he pointed the 9mm at him.

The man's eyes widened. "You'd kill me now?"

"I'd kill you now," Tull said in a flat voice.

"Ashcans, two on the port side!" Hacker shouted.

"Hard left rudder," Smith ordered.

"Hard left rudder," the helmsman answered.

"Take her up five hundred—" Smith stopped. "Surface . . . Surface," he ordered, locking his eyes with Tull's.

Tull nodded and in a quiet voice he said, "We may never get there."

"If we stay down, we don't have a chance," Smith answered.

"Diving planes up fifteen. Blowing all ballast," Bright reported.

Two explosions caught them on the stern, and suddenly lifting it, swung the bow down toward the bottom.

"Christ!" Smith swore, grabbing on to the side of the periscope to steady himself.

Moments changed into minutes before the *C-1*'s bow came up again.

"Go aft and check the shaft seals," Smith said, looking at Tull.

"Aye, aye," Tull answered, relinquishing command to Smith.

Commander Paul Cole, captain of the *Knox*, stood in back of the sonar operator and looked at the sonar display scope.

"They're movin' up fast, sir," the operator said, glancing back over his shoulder at the skipper and the sonar officer.

"You have any dead spots around where they could hide?" he asked, worried that the *C-1* would find a thermocline and suddenly become invisible.

"No sir. No dead spots with the range of equipment," the operator answered.

"They just might be coming all the way up," the sonar officer, Lieutenant (jg) Horace Wiggims the third, ventured to suggest.

Cole looked at his junior officer. "Is that what you really think, Mister Wiggims?" he asked, pushing the man not to back down.

Wiggims shifted his weight from his right foot to his left and, looking toward the sonar display scope, he said, "Sir, they continue to go up. They know we're here. I think they're going to surface, sir."

"So do I, Mister Wiggims . . . so do I," Cole said and, picking up a phone to the CIC, he ordered the fire-control officer to cease firing.

"Yes, Mister President," Maylee said, speaking into the scrambler radio phone, "we have the *C-1* under attack now. We have not been able to raise it on the ELF radio. I radioed our facility in Michigan and my message was then transmitted to the *C-1*. I requested an immediate surrender. There wasn't any answer."

"Is there any possibility that they did not receive your message?" the President asked.

"Yes, sir, there is."

"Is there any other way to signal them?"

"No, Mister President. Our sonar operators have picked up sounds that could only be interpreted as gunfire."

"Gunfire?"

"There's more than a possibility that some of the crew could have tried to regain control of the boat."

There was a slight pause before the President asked, "If that happened and they were successful, how would you know?"

"There would be no way of knowing that, Mister President," Maylee answered.

"Then you could very well be firing—"

"Excuse me, Mister President," Maylee said, "I have just been handed a message from Captain Cole, the skipper of the destroyer *Knox*. The *C-1* appears to be heading for the surface."

The President uttered a sigh of relief. "Cease all firing," he said.

"Yes, sir, Mister President," Maylee answered, aware that Cole had already ordered it.

"I want to know the moment you put your people aboard," the President said.

"Yes, Mister President."

"I want you to have Commanders Tull and Forbushe flown to Washington."

273

"Is there anything else, Mister President?" Maylee asked.

"The *C-1* is to return to home port as soon as possible," the President said.

"Yes, Mister President," Maylee said. "I will keep you informed of the events as they happen here."

"Thank you, Captain Maylee, for a job well done, and express my appreciation to every member of your battle group," the President told him.

"I certainly will," Maylee answered, and as soon as he heard the President click off, he put the phone down and leaning back into his captain's chair, he smiled. His promotion to admiral was assured, or, in the vernacular, it was in the bag.

Benjamin was the first one out of the car, Lotz came next, his secretary, Nemet, followed and Markham was last.

"There's someone watching from behind the blinds on the ground floor," Benjamin said, admiring the house and the grounds around it. He'd always had a fondness for English Tudor. It was class, quietly stated. But class nonetheless.

"That's the study," Lotz said.

"Hubbered?" Markham questioned.

"Yeah, I guess," Benjamin answered; then glancing back at Nemet, he said, "You managed to get a phone call to him, didn't you?"

She didn't answer.

They reached the door and Benjamin rotated the knob, opening the door easily. He turned toward the study and, within a matter of moments, he opened that door too.

Hubbered was standing behind his desk. He was pale and his face was drawn. He said nothing.

"We have two friends of yours here," Benjamin told him, entering the study and followed by the others with him.

"Are you alright, Nemet?" Hubbered asked, starting to go to her. He loved her, that was totally obvious.

"Stay where you are," Markham barked.

"Okay, Mister Hubbered, we know something about your activities," Benjamin said. "Now tell us about—"

Suddenly an intercom came on. "Mister Benjamin and Mister Markham, put your weapons down on the desk. We have your former wife, Mister Benjamin, and we have your girlfriend, Mister Markham," a male voice said.

Benjamin grabbed ahold of Nemet and pushed his .38 against the right side of her head. "And I have her," he shouted, knowing that whoever had spoken would be able to hear him.

"Her life is meaningless to us," the voice said.

"No," Hubbered shouted. "Oh, God, no!"

"He won't harm her," the voice said. "He won't do anything. Look to your right, Mister Benjamin and Mister Markham."

A wall TV suddenly came on. Both Liz and Karin were naked on a bed. Each was spreadeagled and bound.

"We will let you see them being raped," the voice said.

"My God!" Markham exclaimed. "It will—" He

stopped, afraid even to think of what it would do to Karin.

"You see," the voice said, "you haven't anything to bargain with. Put your guns down on the desk."

Benjamin nodded and, lowering his gun, he said, "We've come up with a bum hand."

Suddenly a chopper swooped down onto the front lawn and a voice said, "Hubbered, this is Otis, the house is completely surrounded. We know Detectives Benjamin and Markham are in there. Send them out unharmed."

Benjamin ran to the window and flung it open. "There are ten cars coming up the driveway!" he exclaimed.

"We still have the two women," the voice said.

"It's over for us," Hubbered shouted. "There's no way out."

Markham grabbed ahold of him. "Where are the women?" he yelled.

"Don't—" the voice began.

"In the rec room," Lotz said.

"Hold these guys here," Markham said, and dashed out of the room.

Benjamin waved to the agents piling out of the cars. "Here," he shouted. "Here!"

A dozen men ran toward the door.

And even as Benjamin turned, Hubbered opened his desk drawer, picked up a .22 automatic and, putting the muzzle against his forehead, he squeezed the trigger.

Markham raced down to the rec room. The door

was locked. He shot it open, pushed the door back and saw a man out of the corner of his right eye. Whirling toward the figure, he fired twice.

The man groaned and dropped to the floor.

Markham went to the women. Neither even knew he was there; they had been drugged.

"Bastards!" he shouted.

Benjamin was suddenly at the door.

"Drugged," Markham said, starting to untie the ropes that held Liz.

"Lotz said there are two other guys—Karum and Rashied; they're somewhere in the house."

"I stiffed some guy," Markham said, still working on the ropes. "He's over in the corner on the right side of the room."

Benjamin looked at the body. "That guy is clean-shaven. The two we want have beards."

"Get the ropes off Karin," Markham said.

"Later," Benjamin answered. "They're safe for now. I want those two guys."

Markham was about to object, then realizing Benjamin was right, he changed his mind, stood up and asked, "Where do we start?"

"The guys from the Bureau are upstairs," Benjamin said. "We'll look around down here." He stepped out of the rec room. "There's a door—"

Two shots splintered the door.

Benjamin crashed to the floor.

Markham dropped to his knees and emptied his .38. The shots brought half a dozen men rushing down the steps.

The door was shot to pieces in various places.

An agent pulled it open.

Two bearded men lay crumpled on top of each other, their jackets stained with blood.

Markham stood up, walked slowly over to where Benjamin lay and hunkered down next to him. He heard one of the agents radio for medical assistance.

Benjamin shook his head. "Waste of time," he said, coughing blood. "Almost had it made. Tell Liz we almost had it made." And his head lolled off to one side.

Markham gently gathered him into his arms and wept for a man he hardly knew but had come to love.

"One hundred feet," Bright called out, gasping for air in the smoke-filled control room.

"Stand by to surface," Smith ordered. "All engines stop."

"All engines stop, answered," Tull answered, manning the telephone to the engine room.

"Diving planes zero," Bright reported.

Hacker had already informed Smith of the presence of the destroyer and that a carrier and three of her escorts were "closing fast." All the vessels had been ID'd.

"Fifty feet," Smith reported. "Stand by to open bridge hatch. Open bridge hatch."

Tull and Ho made it up the ladder, undogged the hatch and flung it open. The clean sharp salt scent of fresh sea air filled Tull's lungs.

He switched on the 1MC. "This is Commander Tull. We are dead in the water."

"This is Captain Cole," a voice answered from the destroyer, which was just holding steerage way, "I am sending a boarding party to you."

"Roger," Tull answered; then he added, "We have some wounded and dead here."

"Understood," Cole answered; then he said, "Commander Tull, I have been told by Captain Maylee to advise you that you and Lieutenant Commander Forbushe are to ready yourselves for immediate transportation to Washington."

"Forbushe is dead," Tull replied.

25

The following day, under a hot July sun, the President, his wife, and Markham, Karin and Liz stood at the edge of the open grave in Arlington National Cemetery, where the President insisted Benjamin be buried, and listened to the mournful sound of a bugler blowing taps. At the President's request, Benjamin was buried with full military honors.

Before the first spadeful of dirt was shoveled into the grave, the President stepped forward and said, "I only met this man once, but I found in him the love of truth that made him special." He looked at Liz. "All of us have lost him," he said gently, and took a step backward.

Markham said, "I'd like to say a few words, Mister President."

"Please do."

"I knew Charles Benjamin somewhat longer than you, Mister President, and I spent much of the last few days in his presence. Charles—Chuck, as he preferred to be called—was a brave, dedicated man. I will miss him the rest of my life," Markham said in a strained voice; then borrowing the shovel from one of the gravediggers, he dropped the first spadeful of earth on Benjamin's casket.

The President asked for the shovel and dropped the second.

Markham and Karin watched the late news from the bed in the motel room. The feature story was about the *C-1* and "its miraculous escape from the jaws of death during its highly secret mission." The commentator said, "While the Navy will not permit interviews with any member of the submarine's crew, we were able to find out from sources that wish to remain anonymous that there were several casualties sustained during the highly dangerous mission and that at its center was someone named John Tull, who appears to be a man who has mastered the art of disappearing. We understand that in some strange way two civilian detectives played a vital role in the success of the mission . . ."

Karin sat up. "That's you and Benjamin he's talking about!" she exclaimed.

Markham reached up and pulled her down to him. "So what. It's over and everything is wrapped up. Well, not everything," he said, gently caressing the side of her face with the tips of his fingers. "Take me home to meet your folks and I'll do the same."

"You sure—"

"Yes, I'm sure," he said, taking her in his arms. "I'm sure I love you."

"I love you too," Karin answered, guiding his hand to her breast. "Love me, Guy."

Slowly, Markham eased her down and, enjoying the delicious taste of her lips, he began to caress the rest of her body.

"So you're a mystery man," Louise chided, using the remote control to turn off the TV and pressing herself against Tull's knees.

He was seated in a club chair and she sat on the floor in front him. It was a very domestic scene. He was wearing a pair of blue PJ's and she nothing more than a white diaphanous negligee.

Tull laughed and said, "I came back to you, didn't I. I bet you never expected that to happen."

She rested her arms on his lap. "Is that a question or a statement?" she asked.

"A bit of both."

"Oh, I don't really know. I believed I held a certain interest for you. But, on the other hand, I wasn't completely sure that it was sufficient to bring you back."

Tull slid his hand over her breasts and spanned both nipples between his thumb and pinky. Almost instantly he could feel them grow. "I don't exactly know what's going to happen," he said. "But if it's possible, I'd like to marry you."

"What?" Louise almost leaped to her feet.

"I thought you might like the idea," Tull said, teasing her nipples again. "I never tried it before, have you?"

She shook her head.

"Well?" he questioned.

Louise smiled up at him. "It might be interesting."

"Yes, I think it would be," Tull answered as he bent down and, bringing her face to his, he kissed her passionately on the lips.

Smith and Peggy sat opposite each other in the living room. They had just finished watching the late news on TV.

"Did you know this John Tull?" she asked.

Smith shook his head. He'd never mentioned Tull's name to her. When he had spoken about him, and those times were few and far between, he'd always referred to him as the XO.

"We have to talk," Peggy said.

Smith agreed.

"You first," Peggy told him.

He was going to object, but instead he nodded and said, "I did some thinking while I was away. I don't want our marriage to end. I mean, I want to try again."

Peggy stood up and moved to the window and looked out on the night. "You're a very brave man," she whispered. "I always knew that and I also know that I'm an alky and no man is brave enough nor should he be, to be tied to—"

Smith stood up and, going behind Peggy, he put his arms around her. "You can be helped," he said gently.

She shook her head and softly began to weep.

He turned her toward him. "We can do it together."

"No," she wept. "No. The night you left I was so drunk I wound up in bed with a man I didn't even remember having seen before, in a motel I didn't remember having gone to. I—" Sobbing, she pushed against him to free herself.

Despite his feeling of revulsion and the momentary flash of anger, Smith held on to her. More than ever she needed him. If he let her go now, sooner or later she'd wind up in the street. Smith pursed his lips. This wasn't the kind of life he'd hoped for, but this was what he had. "Listen," he said, gently shaking her to get her to look up at him, "I'd be lying if I told you what you did didn't matter, but it's not the end of the world. I—" He suddenly realized that what he was about to say was true. "I love you, Peggy," he said. "Maybe, if you love me, we can make it work."

"I do love you," she answered.

Smith pressed her to him.

At rigid attention, Tull faced the President in the Oval Office. He wore his service whites and, because his left shoulder was bandaged, he had his beaked cap under his right arm.

"I don't know whether to recommend you for a medal or have you put under arrest," the President said, leaning back in his swivel chair. "What do you think I should do?"

"If our positions were reversed, I'd have the same dilemma," Tull said honestly.

"You ran a grave risk and a number of good men paid with their lives."

285

Tull didn't answer. He was sure the President by now knew the warp and woof of the situation. The Libyans had turned Harry and bought Hubbered for money, and with Hubbered they also threw in a beautiful woman. Forbushe and eight of the impostors were either Libyan agents, or in it, as Pilcher was, for the money.

"And you were personally responsible for the death of several of those men, weren't you?"

"Yes, Mister President."

"And you offer no explanation other than it was necessary for the success of the mission?"

"Sir, I have no explanation. There wasn't any other way to destroy the spy ring and at the same time return *Command One* to its captain and crew."

"I want Commander John Tull out of the Navy," the President said, practically bouncing forward and planting his elbows on the desk. "I will have his name stricken from the record. Is that clear?"

"Yes, sir."

"Find a new name," the President said. "One that you can live with and the rest of us can also. Is that clear?"

"Yes, Mister President. As of this moment, John Tull no longer exists."

TURN TO RICHARD P. HENRICK
FOR THE BEST IN UNDERSEA ACTION!

SILENT WARRIORS (1675, $3.95)

The RED STAR, Russia's newest, most technically advanced submarine, has been dispatched to spearhead a massive nuclear first strike against the U.S. Cut off from all radio contact, the crew of an American attack sub must engage the deadly enemy alone, or witness the explosive end of the world above!

THE PHOENIX ODYSSEY (1789, $3.95)

During a routine War Alert drill, all communications to the U.S.S. PHOENIX suddenly and mysteriously vanish. Deaf to orders cancelling the exercise, in six short hours the PHOENIX will unleash its nuclear arsenal against the Russian mainland!

COUNTERFORCE (2013, $3.95)

In an era of U.S.-Soviet cooperation, a deadly trio of Kremlin war mongers unleashes their ultimate secret weapon: a lone Russian submarine armed with enough nuclear firepower to obliterate the entire U.S. defensive system. As an unsuspecting world races towards the apocalypse, the U.S.S. TRITON must seek out and destroy the undersea killer!

FLIGHT OF THE CONDOR (2139, $3.95)

America's most advanced defensive surveillance satelllite is abandoning its orbit, leaving the U.S. blind and defenseless to a Soviet missile attack. From the depths of the ocean to the threshold of outer space, the stage is set for mankind's ultimate confrontation with nuclear doom!

WHEN DUTY CALLS (2256, $3.95)

An awesome new laser defense system will render the U.S.S.R. untouchable in the event of nuclear attack. Faced with total devastation, America's last hope lies onboard a captured Soviet submarine, as U.S. SEAL team Alpha prepares for a daring assault on Russian soil!

Available wherever paperbacks are sold, or order direct from the Publisher. Send cover price plus 50¢ per copy for mailing and handling to Zebra Books, Dept. 2622, 475 Park Avenue South, New York, N.Y. 10016. Residents of New York, New Jersey and Pennsylvania must include sales tax. DO NOT SEND CASH.

THE FINEST IN SUSPENSE!

THE URSA ULTIMATUM   (2130, $3.95)
by Terry Baxter

In the dead of night, twelve nuclear warheads are smuggled north across the Mexican border to be detonated simultaneously in major cities throughout the U.S. And only a small-town desert lawman stands between a face-less Russian superspy and World War Three!

THE LAST ASSASSIN   (1989, $3.95)
by Daniel Easterman

From New York City to the Middle East, the devastating flames of revolution and terrorism sweep across a world gone mad . . . as the most terrifying conspiracy in the history of mankind is born!

FLOWERS FROM BERLIN   (2060, $4.50)
by Noel Hynd

With the Earth on the brink of World War Two, the Third Reich's deadliest professional killer is dispatched on the most heinous assignment of his murderous career: the assassination of Franklin Delano Roosevelt!

THE BIG NEEDLE   (1921, $2.95)
by Ken Follett

All across Europe, innocent people are being terrorized, homes are destroyed, and dead bodies have become an unnervingly common sight. And the horrors will continue until the most powerful organization on Earth finds Chadwell Carstairs — and kills him!

DOMINATOR   (2118, $3.95)
by James Follett

Two extraordinary men, each driven by dangerously ambiguous loyalties, play out the ultimate nuclear endgame miles above the helpless planet — aboard a hijacked space shuttle called DOMINATOR!

Available wherever paperbacks are sold, or order direct from the Publisher. Send cover price plus 50¢ per copy for mailing and handling to Zebra Books, Dept. 2622, 475 Park Avenue South, New York, N.Y. 10016. Residents of New York, New Jersey and Pennsylvania must include sales tax. DO NOT SEND CASH.